"In *The Last American Star,* E.B. Fletcher tells the story of a great ship wrecked on a far shore. This is a good read for young adults, and my granddaughter, Morgan, especially liked the parts about the famous mystery man on the beach. Fletcher has great talent for writing for young readers. In this book, her story and characters are very interesting and believable, and the reader is incidentally rewarded with lessons in Spanish and in maritime history."

—William A. Fox
Author

"*The Last American Star* is a little different in that it's a children's book that will also appeal to adults. I liked it for several reasons. First it's about my favorite ship, the *America.* Over the years this transatlantic liner has always appealed to young boys, and even in death it attracts the children of Fuerteventura. E.B. Fletcher creatively uses the ship, William Francis Gibbs, and Commodore Anderson's dog Chota Peg to weave together a story that has warmth, drama and a message. I hope you enjoy it as much as I did."

—Larry Driscoll
Author

"Thank you so much for sharing your book entitled, *The Last American Star.* Your important book will help introduce a new generation of readers to one of the nation's great transatlantic liners. You have created a moving portrait of the final days of the fabled American ocean liner, the *America,* and how she met her ignominious end by splitting in two in the pounding surf on a sandbar in the Canary Islands. There is an enduring air of mystery and majesty surrounding this ship as she makes her final ghostly appearance, and you have added depth and texture to the story as a group of local children encounter the 'ghost ship,' each child seeking and finding something different from the mysterious vessel.

"It was a particular pleasure to meet my grandfather, William Francis Gibbs, in your pages. As designer of the *America* and some 6,000 other vessels during the course of his career as a naval architect, he enjoyed a prolific career that is now largely forgotten. I was pleased to see him resurrected in your pages.

"I am happy to endorse your important work and hope that it enjoys a wide readership among children and adults alike."

—Susan L. Gibbs
Granddaughter of S.S. *America*'s designer

"E.B. Fletcher's latest creative effort demonstrates anew that she is not only a talented educator, but also a lady appreciative and understanding of the oft-times unforgiving ways of the sea. *The Last American Star* skillfully utilizes the sad ending of a famous American-designed and built luxury liner—the SS *America*—as the backdrop for an intriguing and inspiring story. Ostensibly a children's book, this is also a fanciful tale with a measure of mystery that also imparts a moral—one that parents and grandparents would do well to revisit and impress upon future generations. All in all, a great read for the young at heart—of any age."

—Bill Lee
(*America's* unofficial historian)

The Last American Star

The Last American Star

Illustrations by William Redd Taylor and Brent Calloway

E. B. Fletcher

VANTAGE PRESS
New York

Cover illustration courtesy of The Mariners' Museum, Newport News, VA. Used by permission.

Photos of W.F. Gibbs used by permission of Gibbs & Cox, Inc. to the extent able to grant.

Published by Vantage Press, Inc.
419 Park Ave. South, New York, NY 10016

Manufactured in the United States of America
ISBN: 0-533-15338-7

Library of Congress Catalog Card No.: 2005907629

0 9 8 7 6 5 4 3 2 1

To all who design, build, crew,
and sail the steel giants of the seas

Contents

Acknowledgments

I would be remiss if I did not thank those wonderful friends who helped this book come to fruition: the late Elizabeth Alexanderson, Larry Driscoll, Kevin Eley, Charlie Finley, Bill Fox, Susan Gibbs, Jeff Henry, Ken Ironside, Bill Lee, Peter Monahan, Bill Taylor, Ralph Freeman, and Brent Calloway.

The Last American Star

One
Danger

"Javier, please bring me more towels!" called his mother in a panicked voice. "The rain is *still* seeping through the front door."

Señora Díaz diligently placed towels around the inside of the door frame to absorb the rain being blown inside. Hurricane-force winds howled continuously around Fuerteventura Island and buffeted the small house. Torrents of rain beat down on the roof and windows. Lightning flashed across the dark night sky as intermittent claps of thunder exploded in violent outbursts.

"I'm glad we closed the outside shutters on all the windows! That's helped to keep some of the water from seeping in," said Tomás Díaz. "The towels are damp around the *ventanas* (ben-tohn'-ahs), but the curtains should be okay."

Tomás was a bright-eyed, even-tempered nine-year-old. He sat in front of the large fireplace stoking the wood to keep the embers dry and continuously glowing. Señora Díaz did not look up from her work yet nodded in agreement at Tomás's comment.

Javier, Señora Díaz's tall and manly seventeen-year-old son, carried an armful of old towels down the narrow wooden stairs and plopped them on the floor beside his mother. He dropped to his knees and began

1

working beside her. They both pressed and jabbed the cotton towels in every crevice they could find. Señora Díaz smiled gratefully at her strong son as he knelt beside her. He reminded her so much of her late husband.

The living room area, normally bright and airy, was dark except for the subtle glow from the numerous candles lit throughout the room. The electricity had gone out hours ago. The candlelight cast long shadows on the stucco walls, making the room appear larger than it really was. Sudden flashes of lightning would erupt outside, causing the whole room to become illuminated and then dim again. The only one who seemed unfazed by the storm was their large dog, Tauben (Tah'-ben). He sat, warm and content, gnawing a bone by the fire, and every so often he would turn a watchful eye on Tomás. Tomás had rescued the large wolfhound stray from a life of foraging, and Tauben, forever thankful, repaid his young master's kindness by protecting him.

Señora Díaz placed the last towel by the front door and sat on her knees. She wiped her forehead with the back of her hand and sighed. "There!"

Javier helped his mother to her feet and said, "Now I guess all we can do is to wait this storm out. I'm going upstairs to get my radio scanner. Maybe I can listen to some reports about this weather. I get a lot of good frequencies at night."

He sprinted up the narrow staircase while his mother walked across the room to the fireplace and knelt beside Tomás. She smoothed his coal-black hair and hugged him gently. Normally he would pull away or complain, but tonight he didn't say a word.

"You've done a wonderful job keeping the *fuego* (foo-ay'-go) going," his mother said. "I see the water is running down the sides of the chimney. It hasn't done that during a storm in a long time."

Tomás replied, "I keep the fire in the middle, away from the dripping water. See?" He looked at his mother with confidence. "I've placed old ashes around the *fuego* to divert the water from it."

"I see," responded his mother. "That was very clever! I'll get some peppers and chicken. We'll roast them on the fire for dinner. Heaven knows when the power will be restored. It's a good thing I had some food reserves."

Javier came down the stairs with his handheld scanner. He flopped down in his father's old chair putting on the headset, adjusting the small frequency dials as if he were some grand radio commander. He listened intently. Señora Díaz came from the kitchen carrying a large wooden bowl with peppers, onions, chicken and skewers in it. She knelt beside Tomás and together they began preparing dinner. Tauben sat by Tomás watching hungrily with his tail wagging in anticipation.

"Hey!" called out Javier. "There's some kind of ship that's in trouble near Fuerteventura."

Señora Díaz turned around and looked worriedly at her son. "Oh my! I certainly hope that it's far out in the Atlantic, or near the African coast, and not in this horrible storm."

"Oh, they're in this storm all right," replied Javier. "The tow line has broken away from some kind of *remolcador* (reh-mawl'-cah-dor) and the ship is adrift."

Señora Díaz turned back to the fire and continued preparing dinner. "What kind of ship is it that needs a tow line?"

Javier sat and continued listening to the headset. "I can't really tell what kind of ship it might be, but if it needs a tow line, it's either broken down or dead."

3

"These January storms are always bad. It seems that as the years pass they are becoming worse and worse around the Canary Islands," said Señora Díaz shaking her head.

The rain began to pour down even harder upon the house. Tomás looked worriedly at his mother and then upward at the ceiling.

She noticed her son's tense expression and said, "Good thing we have a fairly new roof, huh? No leaks so far! We'll be all right, Tomás."

"Will we, Mamá?" he asked.

"Of course we will!" his mother said measuredly. "We will be hot with the *fuego* and no cool air, but we will survive." Javier quietly listened as Tomás sulked.

"I am worried about the clubhouse," confessed Tomás. "I tried to secure everything in it as best I could, but this storm is really bad."

"What do you have that's still out there?" asked Javier. "I told you to bring all of your papers, pencils, and books inside," he scolded.

"I did what you told me," replied Tomás. "Only . . . I forgot my picture of Papá. It is tacked onto one of the walls. It won't blow away, will it, Javier?"

Señora Díaz interjected, "It is too late to worry about that now, Tomás. Javier, see if you can tell from the scanner when this storm will be over."

"There is a lot of static tonight with this storm. It sounds like the tug is somewhere near the Canary Islands, or the northwest coast of Africa, perhaps near our island, Fuerteventura. Boy, the Atlantic Ocean must be rough tonight!"

No sooner were those words out of his mouth when a streak of lightning crackled through the dark, humid sky, shooting an electric finger to the earth, right toward the

Díaz's home. An immanent *boom* followed the lightning streak with another jolt following. It sounded as if a cannon had been set off. Señora Díaz screamed as the thunder echoed overhead. Both boys jumped up and ran to their mother, who was now standing in the middle of the living room. They held on to each other forming a huddle. The whole house shook violently rattling the windowpanes, china and glasses in the cupboards, and causing a picture to tumble from a nearby wall. Tauben let out a long mournful howl and began to bark incessantly.

Señora Díaz quickly released the hold on her children. "Quick, Javier, go upstairs and check the loft!" she said as she grabbed a nearby candlestick. "Here is a light. Watch your step and be careful." She turned and handed another light to Tomás. "Here is one for you. Check the back rooms down here while I look in the kitchen." Señora Díaz went straight to a cupboard and pulled out a kitchen fire extinguisher that she kept for emergencies. After a swift inspection upstairs, Javier reappeared dressed in his yellow rain slicker.

"I don't see any damage upstairs but I'm going outside to check the roof," he announced. "I have my big flashlight. You and Tomás stay in here. I'll be back."

While Javier pulled the hood of his slicker onto his head, Tomás came into the kitchen. "I didn't see anything in the back of the *casa* (k ah' sah). I felt the walls and everything."

"*Gracias* (Gr-ah'-see-ahs), Tomás," said his mother distractedly. She placed the fire extinguisher on the kitchen table. "You go on back to the *fuego* and make sure that it doesn't go out, hmm?" Tomás walked back into the living room and sat down beside Tauben. Tauben was on "red alert." He sat attentively with ears pricked and eyes wide.

"Be careful, Javier," warned his mother. "This storm is wicked. Keep your hood on and make sure that you are covered up good and stay close to the *casa*!"

Javier slowly opened the back door trying to keep the wind at bay, but the change in the air flow caused the door to be sucked wide open hitting the kitchen wall. The open door allowed a flood of rain to pour upon the kitchen floor blowing leaves about the room. Javier struggled with the door. Señora Díaz helped close the door behind him as Javier stepped into the stormy night. Tomás and Tauben sat motionless, waiting. The only sounds present in the house were the ticking of the battery-powered wall clock and the howling wind. Señora Díaz paced back and forth across the kitchen floor. The humidity formed water droplets on her dark skin causing her cotton dress to become damp. Occasionally the bright beam from Javier's flashlight would sweep across the windows and shine through the cracks of the outside shutters. Tomás got up from his place by the fire and peeked out of the living room window straining to see any sign of his brother. Señora Díaz looked at the wall clock, mentally counting the minutes Javier was gone. After what seemed like an eternity, the opening of the back door broke the stillness of the room. Javier quickly stepped inside the hot kitchen and with some effort, closed the door behind him. He was sopping wet. His mother handed him a dry towel and waited for a verdict. Tomás stood in the doorway with Tauben.

"Well?" questioned Tomás anxiously.

"Well—" Javier answered wiping the water from his eyes. "I can't really see if there's any damage to the *casa*. The roof looks okay and there isn't any smoke or fire, but the clubhouse and tree are gone. The lightning hit the tree and it missed hitting the *casa* by inches. It took the lightning's blow. The clubhouse is a charred mass of splintered wood which hardly resembles the structure it once was. I can't even make out where the windows and door were; the flooring has caved in too." Javier cast a concerned glance at his brother as he continued to dry off. Tomás turned around and slowly walked back in the living room, slumping down in front of the fire.

"My picture of Papá is gone then," Tomás solemnly whispered.

"*Gracias,* God. It didn't hit our home," cried Señora Díaz as she lifted the gold cross she always wore and pressed it against her lips. "Your blessed *papá* watches over us. God bless his soul," she said looking upward at the ceiling.

Javier hung up his rain gear to dry and walked into the living room. He patted his mother on her shoulder as he passed. He knelt beside his younger brother. Tomás held several skewers in a kitchen mitt. The long pointed skewers held chunks of peppers, onions, and chicken on them. The food sizzled as it cooked over the fire. Tomás starred at the dancing flames. Javier cast a concerned look at his brother. Tomás felt his brother's stare but was afraid to look at him for fear he would see the tears brimming in his eyes. After a few moments Tomás said, "I guess I'm too big for a clubhouse anyway." Tauben, sensing Tomás's sadness, licked his young master on the cheek.

Javier was unsure whether to call attention to his brother's tears. He sat for a moment pondering and then said, "We'll have a lot of yard work to do once this storm is over. We'll ask my friend Carlos if he can help us. Uncle Antonio will probably help, too." Tomás just gazed blankly into the fire. Just then there was another crash of thunder.

Study Questions for Chapter One

1. Who are the main characters introduced in this chapter?
2. Why are there candles lit inside the house?
3. Describe how the Díaz family coped during the storm.
4. What does it mean on page 2, "He reminded her so much of her late husband." What does "late" mean in this sentence?
5. What are skewers? (On page 3, the family used these to prepare their dinner.)
6. How does Tomás's reaction to the destroyed clubhouse compare or contrast to Javier's reaction?

Activities:

With your parents' and/or teacher's permission, log on to the following Web site, *www.red2000.com / spain / canarias,* and read the information available about the Canary Islands.

1. How many islands are there?
2. What is the capital of the Canary Islands?
3. Which continent are the Canary Islands closest to?
4. How far away do you live from the Canary Islands? (Estimate.)

Extra research: How hard must the wind blow in order to be called "hurricane force"?

Two

Remorse

After a light supper of goat's milk, roasted peppers, and chicken with onions, the little family sat together in the candlelit room. Señora Díaz darned several socks by candlelight, while Javier listened to radio transmissions from the tugboat. Tauben lounged dreamily by the fire, having had his own fill of the chicken, while Tomás practiced his math facts by the firelight. He looked at his mother and asked, "Will we have *escuela* (eh-squay'-lah) tomorrow?"

"I'm sure not," replied his mother. "But, *escuela* or no *escuela,* you finish your math just the same."

Tomás rolled his eyes at his brother, who was mischievously smiling at him from across the room as he lounged in a chair reading.

"Why does Javier not have math to do?" whined Tomás.

"Because he is older and has already learned his facts," stated his mother emphatically.

"It's not fair!" whined Tomás.

"Life is not fair, my son," said Señora Díaz. "Study!"

During the night, the rain subsided. They awoke to silence. The pounding rain and the howling wind had been replaced with a soft light rain, which diminished as the night wore on. At daybreak, the sky was still overcast and the winds were brisk, causing whitecaps on the Atlantic, although the sea was barely visible from their home. The steady hum of chainsaws signaled the cleanup operations from the storm's aftermath.

The Díaz family rose at daybreak with the pounding of a fist on their front door. Tauben barked furiously as Javier cautiously opened it.

"I see that lightning got your tree and clubhouse last night!" said Uncle Antonio. "I couldn't call because the *teléfono* (teh-leh'-foh-noh) lines are down. I'll get some *hombres* (ohm'-brays) together and we'll get that mess cleaned up. Is your mamá all right?"

"*Sí,* (See) she's fine. We all are. Just a little shaken up, that's all," replied Javier.

"Get something to eat and meet me in about an hour. Better get some work gloves. You are going to need them," directed Uncle Antonio as he walked away.

"*Sí,*" replied Javier. He watched his tall, muscular uncle walk across their front yard. Antonio had a slight limp from a sailing accident years before, other than that, the resemblance to Javier's father was striking.

"Who was that?" asked Señora Díaz coming from the kitchen, wiping her hands on a dish towel.

"It was Uncle Antonio," he replied. "He's going to get some fellows together to tear down what is left of the clubhouse and saw up the downed tree."

"Bless him!" cried his mother. "You better get washed up. I'll get some breakfast for you. Be frugal with the *agua* (ah'-gwah)," she reminded him.

"I hope the electricity comes on soon," stated Javier. "Then the lights and well pump will work again!"

"Until then, we must use the water in the pails sparingly," said Señora Díaz.

After a breakfast of potato cakes, orange slices, and

goat cheese, Javier, Tomás and their mother went outside to survey the damage from the storm. Lightning had struck the clubhouse with such force that it had left a huge crater in the earth where the tree hit the ground. The tree, which had housed the clubhouse, lay across the backyard like a fallen giant. Lots of debris lay in the yard. Other than a couple of roofing shingles that had blown away, there was no real damage to their home.

"Now our nerves can rest," said Señora Díaz. She walked around the yard inspecting everything. "Tomás, get some trash bags and a rake. Let's get this garbage out of the yard first," she directed.

"*Sí,*" said Tomás running inside the little house.

Javier went over to the old shed and retrieved his father's work gloves. While Javier waited for Uncle Antonio and the other men, he went back inside and put on the scanner headset. He fiddled with the dials and eventually found transmissions from the tugboat he had listened to the night before. He didn't want to waste too much battery power, but the endangered ship intrigued him. As he listened, he learned that the tugboat was of Ukrainian registry and the crew had been unable to tie a tow line to the adrift ship. There were four crewmen who were being airlifted from the unsecured ship by a search and rescue helicopter.

"Boy!" said Javier out loud. "I would hate to have been one of those guys being tossed around on that ship in the storm! I'll bet they're green with seasickness!"

Tomás came running into the house with a box of trash bags in his hand. Javier called to him, "Hey, dwarf!"

"What?" answered Tomás stopping in his tracks and looking at his brother.

"They're airlifting crewmen from that ship by helicopter!" said Javier.

11

"Wow!" yelled Tomás in reply. "How do you know?"

"I have been listening to their conversations from the tugboat and they seem to be on the other side of Fuerteventura! Come low tide, that ship's surely going to beach!"

"We better hurry!" replied Tomás. "Let's go see it. Puh-leeze?"

"I like it when you beg," chuckled Javier. "After you finish picking up all those twigs, leaves, and stuff, you have got to lock the shutters back in place," reminded Javier. "It is too hot in here! The sooner we get some fresh air circulating the better!"

"I know! I know!" responded Tomás. "What are *you* going to do?"

"I am waiting for Uncle Antonio to come over and help tear down the clubhouse and saw up the tree!"

"Oh!" said Tomás, slowly dragging the trash bags behind him; he turned and walked outside and into the front yard where his mother was waiting for him. Tomás spied Carlos approaching. Javier and Carlos had been close friends for many years. Carlos had broad shoulders and rugged good looks and all the girls hung on his every word. Tomás yelled out from the front yard to his brother, "Here comes Carlos! Tell him 'bout the ship!"

Carlos strolled across the yard and said, "*Hola* (Oh'lah), tell me about what ship?"

By the time Carlos had reached the small front porch of the house, Javier was standing in the front door frame and said, "There is a ship that's broken from its tow line. It is near the island. Looks like she will beach by low tide. Tomás and I are going to see it as soon as we finish our chores. Want to come, too?"

"Sure!" responded Carlos.

"Check out the clubhouse," directed Javier, glancing in the downed tree's direction.

Carlos's eyes became really large. "Man! What happened?"

"Lightning strike," responded Javier.

"You are lucky it didn't hit your *casa*! Do you remember all the times we played in there?" reminisced Carlos. "It is a shame."

"Did you have any damage from last night's storm?" inquired Javier.

"*Sí,*" responded Carlos. "Part of our roof blew away last night! We don't know how we are going to fix it!"

Javier looked surprisingly at his best friend and said, "Man! Much water damage?"

"Yeah," replied Carlos.

"What are you going to do now to keep water out?" asked Javier.

"Right now, we are putting a large tarp on the roof. I came over to ask if you could help to secure it, but I see that you have things to do, too."

Javier thought for a moment and said, "How about if you help me with cleaning up the clubhouse and I will help you with nailing down the roof tarp!"

"With all of this work to do, are you sure we'll have time to go see the ship?" asked Carlos.

"We'll try," replied Javier.

"Deal!" said Carlos punching Javier on the arm.

"I have my papá's old work gloves," said Javier.

"Hey, I have some at the *casa* too!" said Carlos. "I will run over and get them and be right back."

While Carlos was gone to get the gloves, Uncle Antonio showed up with two other men and they all began dismantling the charred remains of the clubhouse and sawing the felled tree. Tomás stayed in the front yard

13

away from the demolition crew. After Tomás finished picking up debris from the front yard, he opened the outside shutters on the windows and reattached them to their outside mounts. Some of the shutters hung crookedly, but they were still intact. Next, he opened all the windows to allow fresh air to flow throughout the house.

Carlos returned with his gloves and helped the crew with the clubhouse. They worked for several hours stacking the salvageable wood from the clubhouse and tree, burning the rest in a large bonfire.

Tomás came around the side of the house dragging four large trash bags filled with the debris from the front yard. He stopped lugging the bags and stood watching the crew working on the clubhouse demolition. Tomás drew in a deep breath and walked slowly over to where his brother was working. "I have done my job!" he announced, looking at the ground. "I have cleaned up the front yard and I opened the outside shutters and all the *ventanas!*"

Javier watched his brother with concern. He stopped stacking wood, brushed the dirt from his shirt and jeans, and walked over to his brother. "Hey," said Javier staring at his younger brother.

"Hey," responded Tomás, still looking at the ground.

"Are you looking for something down there?" teased Javier.

Tomás did not respond. Javier put his arm around his little brother and said, "I know that you are upset, dwarf. There was no saving the clubhouse. You saw what the storm did to it. I'm sorry. We can always build another one."

Tomás looked up at his older brother. He had tears in his eyes. He said in a quiet voice, "We can build another clubhouse, but we can't build another picture of Papá. It's all that we had left from him."

14

Javier stood beside his brother. "I understand," he said. He sighed a long sigh, then looked compassionately at his little brother. His thoughts were racing as to how to handle the situation.

"It's not fair!" interjected Tomás.

"Well, maybe it's not, dwarf," he said, looking back at his brother. "But it's happened and there isn't anything we can do about it."

Tomás just stood looking down at the ground while Javier had an idea. "Hey," Javier said pulling Tomás tightly against him. "Look at the white clouds up there." Tomás looked into the sky. He saw wispy white clouds, the brief remnants of yesterday's storm. "See how they change shapes?" directed Javier. Tomás studied the clouds and slowly nodded his head. "That's sort of like our lives are, I guess. We think our lives are one way and then they suddenly change, becoming something completely different. Sometimes it takes a while for change and then at other times, change comes very quickly." The boys stood watching the sky for several minutes. "Do you see what I mean?"

Tomás nodded his head again. In a few minutes Tomás said, "I see a dolphin," looking at the sky and pointing.

"Where?" asked Javier.

Tomás pointed to a cloud. "There, that cloud!" he said.

"I don't see it!" said Javier, looking and squinting.

"Well, it's really not a dolphin anymore. It kind of looks like a horse now," said Tomás.

"See what I mean?" asked Javier.

"*Sí,*" said Tomás. "I get it."

"You sure?" asked Javier.

"*Sí,* I'm sure," replied Tomás.

15

"It's all right to miss Papá, Tomás," said Javier. "I still miss him, too."

Tomás nodded his head and, looking at Javier, said, "I have to burn all of these trash bags in the pile." Tomás picked up the bags and began lugging them across the backyard.

"Okay," said Javier. "You want some help?"

"I can do it," said Tomás, scowling. "I'm not a *bebé* (beh-beh')."

Uncle Antonio had stopped working and watched Tomás and Javier. He could tell something was up.

"No one said you were a baby," chided Javier. "I know those bags are pretty heavy." Javier watched as Tomás struggled with the bags. He took two manly strides toward his little brother and lifted one of the bags and hoisted it over his shoulder as he walked to the bonfire. "Come over here so we can burn the rubbish," he directed.

"Show off!" called Tomás.

Javier cast a glance toward his brother as he continued walking and said, "You better be nice to me, dwarf, or I will toss *you* in that pile!"

"You will have to catch me first!" said Tomás, dropping his trash bag and running away from his brother. Javier shook his head and chuckled. After he dumped the trash bags in the fire, he walked back to where he had been working. He saw Uncle Antonio watching him.

"Javier!" called Uncle Antonio. "Is everything okay with Tomás?"

"*Sí,*" replied Javier. "He's just upset about the clubhouse. Papá built it for us, you know. He will be all right."

Uncle Antonio nodded at Javier with understanding, then he cast a protective eye toward Tomás, who was now dumping trash into the fire.

"Hey, Uncle," called Javier. "What time is it? I forgot my watch."

His uncle pulled up his cotton shirtsleeve and replied, "A quarter till twelve."

"Gosh!" said Javier. "It is already 11:45! I didn't realize it was so late! We worked almost to *siesta*! I told Carlos I would help him secure a tarp on his roof! We have to get going! We need lots of daylight to get that done!"

His uncle nodded to him and motioned for him to go on, saying, "We will eat after we have finished! You go on! We will meet up with you after *siesta*."

Javier nodded in agreement with his uncle. Then, he motioned to Carlos and Tomás. "Come on! We're going over to Carlos's to help with the roof tarp! Tomás, run in the house and tell Mamá where we are going! And see if the electricity has come on!"

Tomás yelled back, "Wait for me!" He flew into the little house and was gone only seconds. He raced out the front door, down the front porch steps, and across the yard, trying to catch up with his brother. Javier and Carlos walked slowly, intentionally so that Tomás could catch up with them.

Javier heard Tomás's approaching steps and called to him over his right shoulder, "Do we have electricity yet?"

Tomás panted, "Not yet!" as he tried to catch up with his brother.

Study Questions for Chapter Two

1. Compare the storm damage that Javier's family encountered with that of Carlos's family.

2. Why was it important for fresh air to be circulated in the Díaz home after the storm?
3. Javier used the clouds in the sky to teach his brother a lesson. How did Javier teach Tomás his lesson?
4. On page 9, what does "subsided" mean?
5. On page 13, what does "dismantling" mean?
6. Make a prediction: How long will it take to have the electricity restored?

Activities:

With your parents' and/or teacher's permission, log on to the following Web site, *www.spaintour.com/canarias.htm,* and read the information about the history of the islands. Then answer the following questions:

1. The Canary Islands are divided into two regions/areas. From the information you read, explain which islands go with which area or region.
2. Which European country had the most influence on the colonization of the islands? Prove your answers with specific facts.

Three

Explorers

The boys returned home well after five o'clock and were very tired. Their mother had warmed some water and had drawn them a shallow but well-deserved bath in an old tin tub. Since the water was not working yet, Señora Díaz heated five large kettles of water in the fireplace and then poured the steaming water into the tub. Javier soaped up, then Tomás. After they had rinsed, dried off, and gotten into clean clothes, they rested for *siesta*. Later they sat down to a dinner of fish and roasted potatoes. Tauben lay on the floor happily thumping his tail. As the boys devoured their dinner, Javier said, "First thing we'll do tomorrow is drive to the other side of the island and see if we can see that ship! I heard on the radio that she beached last night, but I'm too tired to go see it today. Putting that tarp on Carlos's roof seemed to take forever."

Tomás nodded in agreement, as he had a mouth full of potato. After swallowing, he asked, "We won't have *escuela* tomorrow, will we?"

Señora Díaz came over to the table and placed another piece of fish on Javier's plate. She picked up Tomás's glass and filled it with more canned tomato juice. "Didn't your Uncle Antonio tell you? *La escuela* had some damage from the storm and won't be open for another three days or so. He and several other *hombres* have been asked to help with the repairs."

"All right!" exclaimed Tomás, smiling from ear to ear and giving his brother a high-five.

"You will still practice your math facts, Tomás," commanded his mother. Tomás just rolled his eyes at her. "Stop that!" she said. "You look like you are *loco* when you do that." Javier laughed at his brother. "And *you!*" continued Señora Díaz pointing a finger at Javier. "*You* better work on finishing the job application for the bookstore."

"Yes, Mamá," said Javier, looking guilty.

Tomás laughed at his brother.

"Quiet, dwarf!" Javier growled, "or I won't take you over to the wreck site tomorrow."

Tomás stuck his tongue out as his brother.

Señora Díaz said, "Stop that. Eat your *cena* (szeh'-nah), both of you." She sat down to her dinner, and after a brief prayer she said, "Where has this ship gone aground anyway?"

Javier swallowed and said, "On the other side of the island. Probably near *Playa de Garcey.*"

Señora Díaz said, "Javier, you know that the military base is no place for boys to wander around. They conduct shelling exercises and maneuvers over there. You two could get hurt."

Javier said, "Mamá, we don't know exactly where the ship is or what shape it is in. Besides, those soldiers aren't going to shell the ship!"

"I beg to differ!" interrupted his mother.

Javier continued, "I'll see if I can listen to the tugboat's transmissions and figure out where the ship might be. Besides, it isn't as if I have never been to Playa de Garcey."

"Mamá," said Tomás, giving her his most pitiful look. "Do you not want us to go and see the ship?"

Señora Díaz said, "No, it is not that I do not want you

to go see this ship, but if it is on military property, there could be trouble if you are caught on the grounds without permission. And don't give me that long face. I'm on to you, Tomás."

Javier nudged his brother under the table with his knee to shut him up. "We understand why you want us to be careful, Mamá. I will find out where the ship is, and if it is on the base, I will contact Miguel. He will be able to help us."

Señora Díaz looked at her son and said, "I haven't heard that name in a while. You haven't seen him for some time—well, since you stopped dating his sister!"

"Here we go again," moaned Javier, throwing his napkin on the table.

"I didn't say anything about Saleena," said Señora Díaz looking innocent. Javier cast a look of warning at his mother. "What?" questioned his mother, throwing up her hands. "You get in one little tiff and then *boom!* You break up with her."

Tomás began to giggle. Javier pointed his fork at his brother and said, "You better pipe down, dwarf!"

"Oh, I'm so scared," teased Tomás.

"So sensitive," scolded Señora Díaz, looking at Javier. "I like Saleena."

Javier said, "Could we please talk about something else?"

"Okay, Okay!" said Señora Díaz looking at Tomás and winking. "Back to Miguel. How long has he been at the military base?"

"About four years," said Javier, continuing to eat. "Since he was promoted."

"I had not realized that. I must go see his *mamá*. It has been much too long."

Tomás asked, "How will you talk to Miguel? The *teléfono* is still out."

"That's right!" agreed Señora Díaz. "If Miguel doesn't know you are coming near the base, then he can't help you. You must get word to him somehow."

"He could talk to Saleena!" said Tomás teasingly.

Javier ignored his brother's comment and said, "I'll listen to the tugboat's transmissions and see if I can figure out where the ship is. If not, I'm sure Uncle Antonio can find out for me. Something like this wreck doesn't happen every day on the Canary Islands! I am sure everyone is talking about it!"

"*Sí,* that's true," admitted his mother.

"Anyway, I can drive near the base without getting on military property. All you have to do is follow the road signs. They either direct you to the base itself or down to the beach," stated Javier. "Papá and I went fishing there several times."

Study Questions for Chapter Three

1. Why is Señora Díaz concerned about where the ship is located?
2. Compare/contrast food you eat for dinner to what the Díaz family eats.
3. What does the word "aground" mean on page 20?
4. Why do you think Javier and Saleena aren't friends any longer?
5. How do you think Javier decided to nickname his brother "dwarf"?
6. What did Javier mean by "You better pipe down, dwarf"?

7. Who are the characters that have been introduced since Chapter One?
8. Select a character from the story and list some of their personality traits. Then pair up with a friend and see if they can guess who the character is, based on his or her traits.

Four
Intrigue

In the morning, Tomás, Javier, Carlos, and Tauben climbed into a battered Jeep Wrangler and took off in search of the ship. Javier listened to transmissions from the tugboat the night before and learned that the ship had indeed run aground during low tide. Javier thought it strange that he hadn't heard any radio contacts with the Spanish Coast Guard.

From the highway, the view of the beachfront was barren, deserted, and mountainous. Since the islands were volcanic in origin, it wasn't uncommon to have mountains so near the sea. In the early-morning mist, the boys neared the turn to Playa de Garcey. Road signs were posted that directed drivers away from the military base itself. Javier followed these signs, which led him directly to the beach. The sky was so overcast and gray that even the seagulls were hidden. The wind was brisk, and white-caps rolled wildly atop the ocean's surface. As the Jeep slowly made its way to the beach, the silhouette of a large liner suddenly loomed from the sea. She lay parallel to the beach, with her starboard side facing them. She already had a slight list to port. Javier slowed the Jeep down and sat there looking at the sight before him. The Ukrainian tugboat that had been towing the beached ship was farther out at sea hovering near the wreck.

The liner was old, yet looked graceful and majestic. She was badly weather-beaten. Her hull was painted an odd, sun-worn aqua. The liner's superstructure was a dirt, muted gray. Her only funnel was painted a faded red at its base and black at the capped sampan top. It looked like she had sported two funnels at one time; however, one had been removed. The base of the missing funnel was still visible behind the pilot house. She appeared to be quite long, with pristine lines, proportionate enclosures, and decks. The bow had beached on a sandbar while her stern was left loose. She looked close enough to touch. The ship sat erect and stoically took the sea's fury. Javier became instantly taken with her. He finally said, "She's a mysterious ghost ship."

"It's so spooky-looking," declared Tomás.

"She is so sad," stated Carlos.

"I wonder where she came from?" asked Javier. "Maybe she was a great *transatlántico* at one time!"

"She looks like a lifeless sea creature now," said Carlos.

"I think she looks like a ghost," chimed in Tomás.

Javier parked the Jeep. The boys were very somber and quiet as they stared at the languishing lady in front of them. She seemed to struggle to keep some dignity from the currents that were trying so desperately to claim her.

As Javier looked on, he noticed streaks of rust on her hull which resembled tears staining a very worn and weathered face.

"How long do you suppose she is?" asked Tomás.

"I don't know. Maybe 200 meters?" guessed Javier.

"Man! That's as long as three soccer fields!" exclaimed Tomás.

The boys walked to the beach to get a closer look at

25

the ship, which was about 70 meters away from the beach. Tauben followed close behind. He stood in the surf looking at the ship, then backed away from the wreck and began barking.

"What's wrong, Tauben?" asked Tomás. "Come here, boy. There's nothing that's going to hurt you. It's just a *transatlántico*."

Tauben stood in front of Tomás, staring at the ship. With some coaxing, he sat down and sniffed the air, never taking his eyes from the wreck.

"What is with *him?*" asked Carlos.

"He's never seen a *transatlántico* this close before," explained Tomás.

Javier walked over to Tauben and rubbed his ears. "See, fella," said Javier. "Nothing is going to get you. It's just an old ship. That's all."

"Come on, Tauben, let's run! Come on, boy! Come on!" said Tomás, patting his leg.

Tauben scampered down the beach away from the ship, barking at the surf. "Don't go too far, Tauben," warned Javier. "We're awfully close to the military base."

Tauben threw his head over his shoulder as if to convey to Javier an understanding as his tongue cascaded from his open mouth.

Javier looked at Carlos and said, "Why isn't the Coast Guard out there? Isn't that the tug that was towing her? You would think that they would get some help!"

"Seems odd, doesn't it?" said Carlos. "Let me see your binoculars. Let's get a better look."

Javier handed the binoculars to Carlos. "I wonder who owns that ship. I would say they are pretty angry right now." The binoculars came upon the ship's name, *American Star*.

Javier got out his camera and began to take pictures

of the liner. He snapped her at various angles and distances. While Javier and Carlos engaged in visually observing the ship, Tomás was looking around for his dog. He noticed the dog's paw prints leading up the bench.

"Hey, Javier," yelled Tomás. "I can't find Tauben!"

"What?" asked Javier distractedly. He was busy taking pictures of the ship.

"Tauben's gone!" shouted Tomás. "He's disappeared!"

Javier stopped taking pictures and scanned the beach. "I thought you were going to take him down the *playa* (plah'-yah)!" said Javier. He also noticed the dog's paw prints leading up the beach toward the base. "I told you to watch him," scolded Javier. "Here!" he said, handing Tomás the camera. "Hold this while I go look for him."

Javier scanned the beach with the binoculars. "I think he's up that way," said Carlos, motioning to the north.

Javier jogged up the beach looking for the dog. Javier had gone a good twenty meters when he spotted a man up ahead. The man sat on the beach staring at the ship. He was dressed in spotless snow-white linen. His shirt was neatly tucked into equally white linen pants, which were neatly rolled up to his knees. He wore a battered brimmed hat and small wire-framed glasses. He was tall yet thin and had an aged pale face, which seemed kind and thoughtful. He had a firm chin, a sharp slender nose, and thin lips. It was obvious to Javier that this man was not native to the islands. The man had a unique air about him that was peaceful and serene.

"*Hola, señor,*" said Javier approaching him. The man was slow to react to Javier, yet looked as if he were anticipating this meeting. Javier approached the man and said, "*Hola, señor.*"

The man smiled and rose to meet Javier, dusting

sand from his immaculate clothing. Javier extended a hand to the man. But instead of returning the gesture, the man tipped the brim of his battered hat in reply. However, his right hand remained inside his pants' pocket. "I see that you and the others have come to see the ship," he said.

"*Sí*," replied Javier, letting his hand fall at his side, a bit embarrassed. "I heard the radio transmissions from the tug on my weather radio. I came here to see what kind of ship it was. That was some storm the other night! I guess you lost power, too."

"Depends on the kind of power you mean," replied the man.

"Electrical power," said Javier somewhat taken aback. "What else?"

The man smiled and, tossing his head in the direction of the ship, asked, "What do you think of her?"

"Pretty sad," replied Javier. "It is obvious she has been neglected for years. I don't know how they'll get her off that sandbar."

The man cast a brief glance back to Javier. "They won't! She wasn't designed to take a blow such as that one—especially at her age and with the condition of her hull. Use your binoculars. You will see that there are many stress buckles and fractures throughout the superstructure, from the storm's battering and the impact with the sea floor. One in particular is right behind the funnel. There is an elevator shaft there. It has caused her keel to crack. With the bow aground the stern free, the rough currents will break her and she will separate completely."

Javier looked suspiciously at the man and then cast a critical eye on the wreck. "How long will she have until that happens?" asked Javier.

The old man looked out at the wreck and drew in a

28

deep breath. Then he said, "Within a day or two I would say."

Javier's mouth opened in disbelief. "Then she's dying!" he said.

The old man watched the ship for a while and then replied, "Yes, you are right. She is dying."

Javier detected a great sadness in the man's eyes.

He said, "She looks like she was a beautiful *transatlántico*." The old man stood quietly beside Javier. "It is a shame she'll be destroyed."

The old man finally replied. "That ship may be far from seaworthy, but she will never be taken by the sea without a fight! She has meant too much to too many!"

Javier looked from the man to the ship and then back to the man again. "You seem to know a lot about that liner," he said.

"Yes, I do," replied the old man, nodding.

Javier, suddenly remembering Tauben, said, "Oh! You haven't seen a big dog running around here, have you? I didn't want him to go too far up the beach."

The old man looked down the southern end of the beach and said, "Is that him there?"

Javier squinted in the direction the old man was looking and saw Tauben with Carlos and Tomás.

"Now how did he get back there?" asked Javier. "That *loco* dog! *Gracias, señor.*" Javier began sprinting down the beach.

The old man looked up quickly into the sky as if listening for something, and called out, "You'd better hurry. There is a military helicopter that will be flying by here soon. They won't like your presence," he warned.

"How do you know that?" yelled Javier.

"They have been around all morning," he said.

"*Gracias, señor,*" said Javier, as he continued down

the beach toward Carlos and Tomás. "Hey, guys!" called Javier waving to them. "Let's go."

Tomás and Carlos met up with Javier. Carlos said, "Why do you want to go so soon? We haven't finished taking a roll of pictures yet."

Javier responded, "Helicopters have been around here. An old *gringo* I met on the beach said they had been around all morning. I don't want any trouble!"

"Okay," agreed Carlos, walking toward the Jeep. "But, I didn't see you talking to anybody. I thought you were standing on the *playa* alone." Javier looked at his friend with disbelief.

"Are you *loco*?" questioned Javier. "He's standing right there." As Javier turned to confirm the old man's position, he scanned the beach and saw no one. "Well, he *was* there," said Javier with a quizzical look. He shrugged his shoulders.

Carlos called to Tomás and motioned for him to follow. The boys and Tauben piled into the Jeep. Javier took off in a cloud of whirling sand. As he looked in his rearview mirror, he saw a military helicopter in the distance approaching the shipwreck.

Study Questions for Chapter Four

1. Why are there mountains so near the sea on Fuerteventura, Canary Islands? What are the islands' origins?
2. On the shipwreck model below, label the parts of the ship:
   starboard side
   superstructure
   funnel (smokestack)

Label the Parts of the Ship

Fletcher Collection

1. port side
2. superstructure
3. smokestack (ventilator)
4. deck railing
5. hull plating
6. promenade deck
7. prow
8. pilot house
9. surf
10. forecastle deck
11. port hole
12. bridge

3. Summarize the conversation between Javier and the old man whom he met on the beach at the shipwreck site.

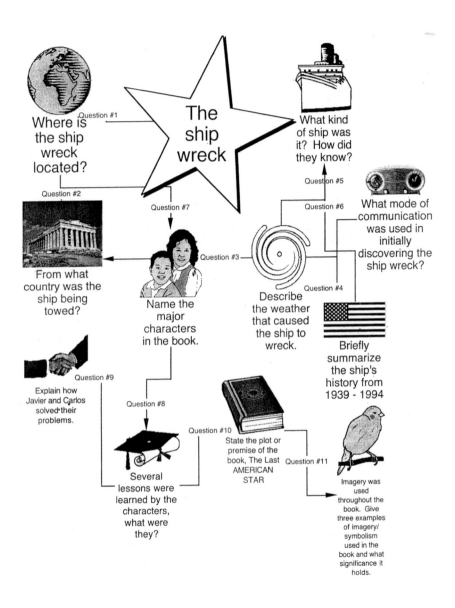

The ship wreck

Question #1 — Where is the ship wreck located?

Question #2 — From what country was the ship being towed?

Question #3 — Name the major characters in the book.

Question #4 — Describe the weather that caused the ship to wreck.

Question #5 — What kind of ship was it? How did they know?

Question #6 — What mode of communication was used in initially discovering the ship wreck?

Question #7

Question #8 — Several lessons were learned by the characters, what were they?

Question #9 — Explain how Javier and Carlos solved their problems.

Question #10 — State the plot or premise of the book, The Last AMERICAN STAR

Question #11 — Imagery was used throughout the book. Give three examples of imagery/symbolism used in the book and what significance it holds.

Briefly summarize the ship's history from 1939 - 1994

Five
Reflections

In the days following their visits to Playa de Garcey, Javier and Tomás talked about the shipwreck incessantly. They wanted to find out where she came from, how she got to the Canary Islands, why she was under tow, and, of course, how old she really was. Javier had continued to take photos of the ship; however, since school was back in session, there was extra homework to do every night. With this extra work, plus beginning his new job at the bookstore, visiting the wreck had taken a backseat. One day after school, Javier was walking home, when his friend Carlos called to him. Javier waited for his friend to catch up. As Carlos approached, Javier asked, "How's the tarp holding up on your roof?"

"My stepdad's getting some scrap lumber together to fix it, but it's going to take a while. We just hope that we don't have another bad storm while we're waiting to get everything together," said Carlos.

"I am sorry that the storm ruined your roof and that water messed up your house. If there's anything I can do to help you, I will," said Javier.

"*Gracias.* You helped out already. If it weren't for you, the tarp wouldn't be on there as well as it is now," said Carlos.

"No problem," said Javier.

"Say, I have heard several of the guys at school talking about the wrecked liner. Did you know that people have been going out and actually getting on it?" asked Carlos.

"I can't believe that," said Javier.

"You know she broke in half."

"I know," replied Javier. "I heard about it. I can't believe the military is letting people go aboard her. You remember that helicopter that checked us out?"

"Sure do," stated Carlos. "From what I hear, the military is casting a blind eye on the islanders who want to go aboard the ship. They figure it's not really their problem, so it seems they really don't care what happens to it."

"You don't say," said Javier.

"*Sí,*" continued Carlos.

"Who owns it?" asked Javier.

"Search me," said Carlos.

"Her name gets me," said Javier.

"*American Star*—kind of a fallen star, now, I guess," said Carlos. "I suppose you could say she's a fallen star."

"Then maybe that makes her the *last American Star,*" declared Javier.

"Indeed," said Carlos.

"Why are people going on her anyway?" asked Javier.

"Same reason we've all been to see her; she's a mystery. Some are going on the wreck, just to explore and look around. Others are taking stuff in hopes of selling it," said Carlos.

"What kind of stuff?" asked Javier.

"Oh, silverware, china, linens, furniture, books—you name it!"

"So they're looting her?"

"*Sí,* I guess you could call it that," said Carlos.

"Man, that's like taking jewelry off a dead body. What are they thinking?"

"Well, so far no one has really claimed ownership of her and she's just sitting out there—so what else *is* there? Let's face it; she's a gold mine just sitting out there."

"I can't believe your attitude," said Javier, staring at Carlos with disbelief. "What these guys are doing is stealing. You can call it whatever you like, but it *is* stealing."

"It isn't stealing if you just go aboard to look and explore, Javier," said Carlos. "Think of it as a wake."

"A wake?"

"Well, you compared her to a dead body, so think of everyone going aboard her as a sort of good-bye."

"Man, you better go to confession soon," chided Javier. "I'll have no part in looting that ship," he stated defiantly. "She isn't our property. It isn't right."

"Relax, man," said Carlos. "Who said you had to *take* anything? I am going to go on her just to look around. Why don't you and Tomás think about coming with me and the rest of the guys on Saturday? There is no harm in that, is there?"

"I have to help my uncle with the goats Saturday morning," said Javier.

"If you and Tomás get up real early, then you could be finished in time to meet us and go on the ship."

"What time were you all thinking about meeting on Saturday?"

"Around ten or ten-thirty," said Carlos.

"I suppose I had better go along to keep you guys honest," said Javier.

"You know, Javier, it isn't a crime to go aboard and just look around. Heck, even the big cruise liners let people go aboard them."

Javier smiled and nodded his head. When he got

home, he talked over the excursion with his younger brother. Tomás couldn't wait to go. Javier warned him about how dangerous it could be and that their mother would not approve. Javier explained to Tomás about the looting and Tomás promised that he wouldn't take anything. They made a pact not to tell their mother where they were going.

On Saturday morning, the boys rose early and completed their chores at Uncle Antonio's farm. Then they drove to the shipwreck. Javier had finally gotten a call through to his friend Miguel at the military base. The phones had just been repaired since last month's storm. Miguel told Javier that if there were any trouble, he would help him. Miguel confided that the military wasn't thrilled about having the wreck so close to the base, but since the islanders weren't really bothering them, the military looked the other way about stripping the wreck.

The weather was typical for the islands—warm with pleasant ocean breezes. The boys pulled up on the beach front. Tomás let Tauben out to run. It was now March and the weather was much calmer than the last visit to the ship two weeks before. Tauben chased seagulls on the wide expanse of sand. There were several islanders on the beach already. Some had tools, ropes, flashlights, or rafts and were clearly bound for the ship; others lounged on the shore soaking up the sun's rays. The rest walked the beach, stopping now and again to stare at the lifeless ship.

Carlos was already on the beach talking with some people when the boys arrived. He spotted Javier and Tomás and waved to them. He then sprinted up to Javier and said, "Hey! Are you ready to go aboard with us?"

"I am!" shouted Tomás.

Javier looked at his little brother and said, "You are not going anywhere just yet, dwarf!"

Tomás stuffed his hands into his jeans pockets, lowered his head, and mumbled under his breath.

Carlos said, "Don't worry, Javier. We're going on the liner just to look around. I told the others how you feel about looting her, and they are going to stay far away from you so that you don't see them take anything. See those crude welded ladders on the side of the hull?" Javier squinted to see the ladders and then nodded his head. "That's how we can get aboard her."

"We've got to climb all the way up there?" exclaimed Javier. "What if someone falls?"

"Just be careful," said Carlos, unfazed. "Nobody's going to get hurt if they're careful. Some of the guys have been out here working on the bottom rung of the ladders. The ladders are usually bent downward to keep people from climbing aboard, so they are using portable torches to alter their configuration."

"I brought a flashlight and some rope, too," said Javier.

"Good. We've brought some ropes and other equipment as well."

"Tomás looked around and said, "Javier, don't look now, but I think Tauben's run off again!"

Javier looked around and said, "Man! Where has that *perro* (peh'roh) gone now?"

Tomás said, "I will go look for him."

"No!" replied Javier. "You stay with Carlos. *I* will get him."

Carlos said, "Tomás, come on down here and meet everyone. We'll get our gear ready." Javier began scanning the beach in search of the dog. He walked north as he did the last time Tauben decided to wander off. Farther up the beach, Javier saw a dog that resembled Tauben. He was sitting beside someone. Javier began to jog in their direction. As he got closer, Javier yelled for Tauben. The dog looked in Javier's direction but remained seated.

"That blasted *perro!*" said Javier under his breath. Javier drew closer and saw that Tauben was sitting beside the old man whom he had met before. The man gently stroked the dog's shaggy coat and Tauben's heavy panting indicated he was enjoying the attention. Javier said, *"Hola, señor."*

Tauben wagged his tail yet remained seated. The man smiled at Javier and tipped his battered hat.

"I hope Tauben hasn't been bothering you. He usually doesn't have much to do with strangers."

"He got away from you the last time we met, didn't he?" asked the old man.

"Sí," answered Javier sheepishly.

The man chuckled slightly at Javier's response and said, "I have been enjoying his company, but I think he came over to check out Chota." The old man tossed his head toward a cocker spaniel sitting next to him. The dog sat perfectly still, watching him with bright button eyes.

"Oh, *señor,* he's a beauty," said Javier. "Is he yours?"

The old man looked out over the wreck and said, "No. He belongs to an old friend of mine who used to sail ships. He is just staying with me for a while."

"What kind of ships did your friend used to sail?" asked Javier.

"Liners mostly," replied the man.

"Like the *American Star?*" asked Javier, tossing his head in the direction of the ship.

"Yes," stated the man. "That exact ship, as a matter of fact."

"No kidding!" answered Javier.

"What's the dog's name again?" questioned Javier.

"Chota," replied the old man. "Chota Peg. It means 'small drink.'"

"That is an interesting name," said Javier. "I suppose your friend named him."

"Yes, yes, many years ago."

"How old is Chota?" inquired Javier. "I mean, the ship looks so old, yet Chota looks so young."

"Let's just say that Chota is a *very* old sea dog," replied the man.

"Funny," said Javier. "He doesn't look old. I suppose he didn't stay on the ship very long."

"I see you have returned with friends," said the old man, changing the subject. "Your dog and I have sat here watching all the activity around the shipwreck." He gently rubbed Tauben's ears. Tauben sat still and seemed to enjoy the old man's attention.

"*Gracias* for warning me about the helicopter," said Javier. "You know, the one you warned me about the last time I saw you here."

"You have been to see the ship since then," stated the man.

"*Si*, but I just sat in the Jeep. I didn't even get out and walk around," replied Javier. "I *have* taken many pictures of it though."

"I see," stated the man.

"Is she an American ship?" asked Javier.

"She was at one time," replied the old man. "She has represented several countries and has been named several times in her career as a liner."

"Like what?" asked Javier.

"Well, first she was named *America*. Then, she was a troop transport during the Second World War named the

USS *West Point*. Next, she returned to her former name and then she was sold years later to Chandris Lines.

"How did she end up here?" asked Javier.

"She had just been sold again and was being towed from Greece to Thailand to be used as a floating hotel. She wasn't given clearance to use the Suez Canal, so they had to tow her around Africa. The rest you know," said the old man.

"This is her final resting place," said Javier.

"Unfortunately, you are correct," agreed the man. "She is a long way from her birthplace."

"Birthplace?" questioned Javier.

"Virginia," answered the man. "Newport News, Virginia."

"Virginia," repeated Javier. "Is that in the United States?"

The old man nodded his head and said, "Yes, it is."

Javier paused for a moment and then added, "This *is* a long way from home. I hear people have been looting her."

"They have," stated the old man.

"It is not right!" declared Javier.

"Shipwrecks have fascinated men for centuries!" said the old man. "I suppose looting them is part of that fascination. Doesn't seem to matter if the ships are below the sea or not, they will be pillaged."

"That still doesn't make it right," Javier replied.

"I agree with you, my lad," stated the old man. "All of her memorabilia is aboard, but it will all soon be gone."

"Memorabilia?" asked Javier. "Like maps, charts, and things like that?"

Again the old man nodded in confirmation.

"My friend and I talked about the looting. There are a

lot of things aboard her. You are probably right," agreed Javier.

The old man arched his eyebrows and said, "The islanders will strip her to the keel."

"Well, *I* am an islander and *I* don't think it is right!" corrected Javier.

"You are different, my boy," said the old man staring into Javier's coal-black eyes. "You have heart and vision."

Javier could feel chills inching up his spine. He was taken aback by the old man's response. He did not say anything for a moment, then he changed the subject. "You were right about the separation of the hull. You said that it would split. I came down to see the ship the day after I met you. The hull had broken by then."

"Umm," said the old man looking away from the ship and stroking the head of Tauben, who now lay at his feet. "The stern section is unstable. It won't last very long. The bulkheads will eventually give way to the sea, and it will submerge."

"What about the bow?" asked Javier.

"It is well aground in the sandbar," replied the old man. "It will eventually be worn away by the sea current, but it will remain longer."

"It still bothers me that the Coast Guard didn't do something to help before it was too late. You would think they would have done *something*!" said Javier. "I was listening to my scanner when the ship beached here. I thought it odd I never heard a call to the Spanish Coast Guard."

"They could not do anything because they were never summoned." The old man sneered sarcastically.

"What do you mean?" questioned Javier with very narrowed eyes.

"Just what I said!" exclaimed the old man. "You seem

like a bright boy. Look at the facts. The *American Star* had to be made seaworthy at an Athens shipyard before ever leaving Greece. She was not given permission to pass through the Suez Canal. She was towed through a violent storm, which I may add, had been predicted. The ship's anchor chain broke in the storm; therefore, the tug's crew removed the four men from the adrift ship. The ship beached on a military base, which has for all practical purposes claimed the wreck as its property. The tugboat, by the way, was seen days after the wreck, cruising the Straits of Gibraltar. Look at the facts."

"Man! Gibraltar is hundreds of kilometers away from here," said Javier as he stepped back from the man with a look of horror on his face and a sudden dawn of realization. "They did not care what happened to her!" exclaimed Javier. "All they wanted is the insurance money from her!"

"I guess some could say that I did not really care," replied the old man under his breath. "I never thought something like this would happen to her. Oh, I knew it was possible—just not probable. She was always so dependable, self-reliant, assured. She never needed me to watch over her. I became so enraptured with the younger one, I completely neglected *her*. Now that she is the one who needs me most, what can I offer?"

Javier watched the man in amazement. The man's teeth were clenched, and he seemed very distraught. The man rose from the beach, wiped sand from his crisp white pants, and said in a low voice, "I will be on my way. If you and your friends are going over to the ship, do so before high tide. The currents are very bad here. The back of the ship is acting as a breakwater right now, but the currents are still treacherous. They will claim even the best swimmer. Some will lose their lives swimming out to the wreck. See that yours isn't one of them."

Javier stepped back from the old man and said, *"Muchas gracias."*

The old man smiled at Javier and adjusted his wire glasses. He started down the beach toward the military base. Chota Peg was already running ahead of him. Javier thought it strange how both dogs had been so calm around the man and that Chota Peg hadn't made a sound. Tauben sat up and stretched. He acted as if he had just come out from under a deep hypnotic trance. He sat on the beach for a moment, sniffed the sea air, and then took off in search of Tomás. Javier yelled, "Hey, wait for me!" He looked over his shoulder for the old man. But just as before, the old man and dark spaniel were gone. Javier also realized that the only footprints on the beach were his own.

Study Questions for Chapter Five

1. What happened to Carlos's house during the storm?
2. Based on what you have read so far, and what you have learned about the Canary Islands, describe the economic base of the characters in the story.
3. Use context clues to define the word, "looting" on page 34.
4. Javier compares looting the ship to taking jewelry from a dead body. What does he mean by this comparison?
5. Chota Peg's name translated to English means

"small drink." Why do you think this name was chosen for the dog?

6. Match the Spanish words to the English meanings below:

playa	school
gracias	beach
senor	thank you
loco	mister
barco	yes
hola	crazy
sí	boat
ventanas	fire
fuego	house
casa	window
escuela	hello

Six
Embarkation

Carlos looked up the beach and cupped his hands around his mouth and yelled, "Come on, Javier! Are you coming or not?"

Javier nodded at his friend and jogged to meet up with him. When he finally caught up with Carlos, he said, "Sorry it took me so long."

Carlos and the rest of the group had gotten a small boat ready to take out to the wreck as they began to plan their day. Javier asked, "What time is it?"

Carlos glanced at his watch and said, "One o'clock. You were gone a long time."

"Sorry," said Javier again. "I don't want to be on the wreck when high tide comes in. You can stay if you want, but Tomás and I will be out of there."

"You have about an hour and a half then," said Carlos. "It will take at least thirty minutes to get on the wreck, so we better not waste any more time!"

Javier nodded in agreement. He looked at Tomás and said, "I don't want you thinking it's okay to deceive Mamá. Before we go home, we will go to the Paraja (Pa-rah'-ha) Bridge and do a little fishing. Mamá thinks that's what we have done this morning. Understand?"

"I understand," said Tomás, smiling at his brother.

As Javier and Tomás got a flashlight, bottled water,

and some ropes out of the Jeep, Carlos walked over to them with an aged brochure that had a cutaway model of the ship. "Look what I've got!" Carlos said, holding the yellowed paper up in the air. "This will show us where we can go on the ship."

"Where did you get this?" inquired Javier, eyeing him suspiciously.

"Don't ask and I won't tell," replied Carlos. "Come on. Time is slipping away."

The boys placed Tauben in the small boat and waded out to the bow section of the wreck. They were careful of their footing as they waded along in the shallow yet strong water. Tauben barked at Javier and Tomás as they guided the boat toward the hull and secured it. "Tauben will stay in the boat," said Javier. "If he gets tired, he'll go to sleep. The rocking motion of the boat always has that effect on him."

Javier instructed his little brother to keep looking upward as he climbed the ladder. Javier didn't want Tomás becoming frightened of the height. Beginning their ascent, Javier noticed great flakes of paint molting from the ship's side. There were hints of other muted colors bleeding through an aqua blue hull. Some pieces were blue, others were white, while still more were black and gray. It was as if, with the various layers of colored paint, the ship was revealing *who* she had been rather than *what* she now was. Once they had climbed the crude ladder, they entered the ship through the glassless promenade deck windows. The years of outward neglect were even worse up close. The teak decking was rotted in places and stained with years of sun-baked pigeon dung. The flooring near the break had caused some outer decks to collapse. The boys found their way to what had been the first-class lounge. The intricate murals and paintings still there were damaged. The room had a mournful echo. Javier stood within the ruins of this once-proud ship, taking in what was left of her. His eyes studied every detail of the room. It was quite large and had a mezzanine above the lounge area. Two massive, ornate doors still hung in the entrance way. They were crafted of heavy bronze with beautiful glass insets. Javier wondered which of the well-to-do passengers had graced this room upon entering through those doors.

"I wonder what this room looked like before," he said aloud.

Tomás stood beside his brother and said, "Before what?"

"Before—the islanders took things. Before—you know, when she was new."

"Oh," said Tomás.

"This is the saddest thing I believe I have ever seen," said Javier sadly.

"What's so sad?" asked one of the boys in the group. "It is just an old ship! It's not like it's a person or something! Geez!"

As Javier stood taking in the room, he slowly countered, "You are wrong."

The boys just shook their heads at Javier and motioned for others to follow.

Carlos stopped and said, "Javier, are you coming?"

"You go on. We'll catch up. I want to look around in here a bit," he replied.

Carlos nodded to his friend and took off after the others. While Javier and Tomás stood in the room, a gentle breeze rustled the still air. Javier wandered around the room, looking at its design and outline. "Be careful where you step," Javier warned his brother. "This part of the ship seems like it's stable, but you can't tell."

"Okay, Javier," answered Tomás.

The curtains, which still hung loosely around the once grand room, swayed with the gentle sea breeze. As Javier walked about the room, he took in the remnants of what seemed to be a luxury hotel. Gradually he began to hear subtle sounds. The sounds were of voices—human voices. They were caught in a sort of hum. The kind of hum you hear when in a large crowd. There were feminine and male voices alike. He couldn't quite make them out. What were they saying? They were soft and gentle. There was laughter. He strained to make sense of what he was hearing. He stepped back and studied the room from different angles. The voices were a blend of sounds. Javier tried to visualize where the voices were coming from and, more importantly, from whom. As Javier walked through the room, he became aware that the voices were those of passengers. Passengers who had once sailed on this grand lady. Their pleasant conversations were a commingle of their days spent at sea, shops they had visited, cities they waited to see, loved ones they had left behind, and again, there was laughter. The soft clinking of crystal goblets, chairs scooting away from tables, silver utensils touching fine china and the wonderful aromas of delectable dishes gave Javier a peaceful feeling. He felt as if he were suddenly a part of a magical transformation. He was unaware that he was smiling until he was abruptly brought back to the present with the slamming of one of the massive bronze doors. Both Javier and Tomás jumped while looking in the direction of the doors themselves. The subtle hum ceased.

Carlos came flying into the room and said, "Come on. Let's go to the cocktail lounge." Tomás and Javier looked at one another with relief. "We've found some fancy artwork on the ceiling back there." The cocktail lounge was

immediately forward of the structural break and was exposed to the elements. Here the ship smelled of oil, mildew, rotten wood, and foul water. The carpeting in some areas was wet, and it squished when walked upon. Javier sighed as his eyes studied the beautiful intricate artwork overhead. He wondered who had taken the time to create such loveliness.

One of the boys called out, "Let's go into some of the staterooms—then on up to the bridge!" They followed Carlos as he led them through various corridors. They stopped and peaked into several staterooms. Most of the rooms had been dismantled. Mattresses were against bulkheads or laying strewn through the corridors. Empty bed frames, broken dishes, postcards, linen, lamps, magazines, and towels littered the passageways. Overturned chairs, tables and glassware were cast about as if the aftermath of a violent brawl; even some of the porthole windows had been removed, leaving massive holes in the bulkheads. The ship's corridors were dark, and with all of the debris, the boys were careful to use their flashlights as they maneuvered their way through the ship.

Once on the bridge, the boys could see the hills beyond the seashore. They watched a few people walking along the beach. The bridge itself was in no better condition than the rest of the ship. Looking down on the forecastle and well decks, the corrosion was heart-wrenching. The ship's list to port was very evident as the group found themselves leaning more toward their left sides. What equipment was still left on the bridge was damaged or broken. The engine telegraph was gone. Charts and other important-looking papers were scattered about the deck as well as broken glass from the wheelhouse windows.

Tomás looked at Javier and said, "I wonder who was

the captain of this ship. Just think, he must have stood here, telling everyone what to do!"

Javier smiled at his brother and said, "Whoever they were, I'll bet they have stories to tell! And, I imagine, they were men of great integrity."

"Lots of stories," echoed Tomás.

"I wonder who designed her," mused Javier while stooping over to retrieve a folder from the mass of papers strewn around the deck.

"What do you mean?" inquired Tomás.

"Well—" continued Javier, flipping through the folder. "There are these fellows called naval architects. They design these ships just like other men design houses and buildings. It's pretty cool to think of somebody creating something like this in their head, drawing it on paper and then having it built. But, best of all, watching it sail!"

"What do you call a place that builds a ship?" asked Tomás.

"A shipyard company, dwarf. You know, like in Algeciras, Spain."

Javier gingerly leaned over and picked up another set of papers and began thumbing through them. He stood there for a good while scanning the papers. Javier and Tomás walked onto the bridge wing and watched the rest of the boys climb atop the pilot house. They all studied parts of the ship. One particular curiosity was the ship's whistle, which was on the smokestack.

"Javier, why do ships have whistles?" inquired Tomás.

"Ship's whistles are their voices," explained Javier. "Whistles announce a ship's arrival or departure from a given port."

"What sound do you think she had?"

"Beats me," answered Javier.

"How do the whistles work?" asked Tomás.

"This ship's whistle was probably powered by steam. That's why it's attached to the smokestack."

"How come ships are called she or her?" continued Tomás.

"You are sure full of questions today, aren't you?"

"Well?" said Tomás waiting for an answer.

"I don't know, dwarf. Maybe because ships have to have a lot of maintenance, like women do. You know how women wear makeup, special clothes, and stuff like that."

"Ships don't wear clothes," said Tomás.

"No kidding!" chided Javier. "They have to have overhauls once a year where they have to go and have new paint and lots of things done to them that's expensive."

Javier strolled back into the wheelhouse and began studying the faded charts that had been tossed about. As he thumbed through a chart, he was gradually aware of muffled noises. These noises were barely recognizable at first, but then they became louder—he heard the pounding of steam engines, commanding voices, and gunfire. Javier bolted from the wheelhouse onto the bridge, expecting to see military troops on the beach. His heart was pounding as he scanned the beach; then he saw the old man dressed in white. He strained to look at him. Javier waved to him, and he waved back. The old man motioned to Javier. Javier squinted and held his hand above his forehead to block the sun's glare. The old man pointed at the boys on the pilot house. Javier shrugged his shoulders at the man. The old man then looked at his wrist. Javier realized that the old man was directing him to the time.

"What time is it?" asked Javier as he stepped back into the wheelhouse.

Tomás looked at his watch, "It's two-thirty."

"We have to go," said Javier to his brother. "The tide will be coming in soon."

"We just got here!" complained Tomás.

"Look, dwarf, it takes thirty minutes to get out here and thirty minutes to get back. There is an hour's time right there."

Carlos stayed with the others while Tomás and Javier retraced their steps through the ship and back down the ladder. Five little boats bobbed on the water below them. The tide was definitely coming in although they could still walk back to the beach. The boys inched down the ladder to their awaiting boat, which contained a refreshed Tauben. He sat up and barked his greetings. Tomás rode in the boat while Javier towed them back to the beach. As they made their way, Tomás jabbered on about all of the things they had seen. Once they were back on the beach, Javier let go of Tauben as he raced around the beach chasing seagulls. The boys beached the boat and then climbed in the Jeep. Tauben, not wanting to be left behind, scrambled into the backrest. As the boys drove away from the beach, Tauben sat holding his head up high so as to catch the full impact of the wind as they jostled to and fro on the bumpy road leading to the main highway.

"Don't forget, we have got to stop and get at least one fish before we go home," warned Javier over the wind.

"Right," agreed Tomás.

After stopping for some bait, the boys drove to the Paraja Bridge and did some fishing with the poles they kept in the Jeep. They caught four fish and arrived at their home later that afternoon. Walking into the kitchen, they presented their mother with the "catch of the day." Tauben took his usual awkward place under the kitchen table, lapping up as much water as he could hold from his large bowl.

Señora Díaz cast an amusing eye on her boys as she washed dishes in a large tub. "My, you have been fishing all this time and you got only four *peces* (pace-ace)? You even fished through *siesta*!" she said. "Javier, you did promise your uncle that you would help him with the goats again this afternoon!"

"I remember, Mamá," said Javier. "I went early this morning and am on my way there now." Javier started for the kitchen door.

"Javier," called his mother.

Javier stopped and looked back at his mother. "*Sí?*"

"Please clean up the floor where Tauben has dribbled water all over it. You would think he hasn't had a drop of water to drink all day."

Javier shot a look at his brother and Tomás's eyes grew wide. "I'll clean it up," said Tomás. "He's my dog."

"We'll go over to Uncle Antonio's," said Javier.

"It is *siesta*!" said his mother. "You know that Uncle Antonio won't be ready until after five o'clock. Where is your head, my son?"

"I don't know," said Javier. "I guess I am not thinking."

"Come sit down and tell me what you two did today," said Mamá slyly.

Javier stood perfectly still, casting a questioning eye at Tomás. Tomás's eyes became wide again and he shrugged his shoulders as if to say, "I didn't do anything."

"Well—" began Javier, holding his brother's gaze, "We went fishing."

"*Sí*, I know," responded his mother. "Why don't you sit down and I will prepare something for you. I'm sure you haven't eaten. Then you can tell me what you saw on the ship."

"Ship?" questioned Javier, looking shocked.

"*Sí*," said his mother as she prepared their lunches. "You know, the one on the other side of the island? The one that is making my children keep things from me."

Javier cautiously sat down. He shot a look at Tomás, and he quickly followed suit and sat down beside his brother. "I do not understand," he said.

His mother looked at him with laughing eyes and said, "You think I don't know where my boys go or what they do? I know where you two were this morning."

"You do?" questioned Javier.

"Um hum," replied his mother, placing apple slices on two plates.

"Are you mad we went to the *transatlántico*?" questioned Javier.

"Dogs get mad. Mamás get angry," corrected their mother.

"A little angry," said Mother thoughtfully. "I know that the ship is at Playa de Garcey and that makes me nervous, but it is fine as long as Miguel knows you are there."

"Then we don't get it?" questioned Tomás looking puzzled.

"Miguel knew we were there. I contacted him yesterday," argued Javier.

"I don't want my boys telling me half-truths," she said, placing plates of fresh tuna and apple slices in front of them. "I know things have been different since Papá died," she confessed, sitting down across from them at the table. "His death has made me realize a lot of things. Like you both keeping things from me. We are all that each other has now. I don't care how good or bad something is, you must tell me things. Understand?"

"We understand," said Javier looking at Tomás. "We're sorry."

"Now," said their mother. "You all have been chatting so much about this *transatlántico* for the last few months that I decided to ask my *amiga* Maria to do some research on it."

"Maria, who works at the book store in Puerto Del Rosary?" asked Javier.

"*Sí,*" answered Señora Díaz. "When you get back from helping Uncle with the goats, I will have a surprise for you!"

"What is it?" questioned both boys at once. They looked at each other, trying to see if the other knew anything about the surprise.

"Maria came to our store a few days ago. She didn't say a word," said Javier.

"You both go wash up and put on clean shirts," commanded their mother with a smile. "You smell like the bottom of a *barco* (bar'-ko). There is water in your pitchers upstairs."

Javier and Tomás looked at one another and began to laugh. They bolted up the stairs. After lunch, they rested and then went to their uncle's to help with his goat farm. They thought about their mother's surprise for them the whole time they were helping repair fences and tattooing several new goats. Javier and Tomás ran home after finishing their chores. They raced each other through the yard and up the steps of the back porch. Their mother was in the kitchen preparing the fish they had caught. As she worked, she softly sang to herself. Javier and Tomás stopped at the door and listened.

"Mamá's singing!" announced Tomás.

"*Sí,*" said Javier, grinning. "I haven't heard her sing since Papá died."

"Me either," exclaimed Tomás.

"Well, it is about time," declared Javier. "Papá has been gone almost two years."

The boys slowly strolled into the kitchen and looked at their mother. Tauben had already heard the boys approaching and sat up with his head cocked, looking puzzled at them. The boys came through the doorway. Tauben announced their arrival with an array of barks while Tomás walked over and lovingly embraced his dog.

Javier wandered over to his mother and gently kissed her on the cheek. "*Hola,* little canary," he said.

Señora Díaz didn't even take a look at Javier as she said, "Go wash up! You now smell like goats!" Javier laughed and motioned to his brother to follow him upstairs to clean up once again.

The boys returned to the kitchen and sat down looking anxiously at their mother.

"Well?" Tomás said, looking alert.

"Well, what?" asked his mother, wiping her hands on her apron. Tomás looked at Javier. Javier laughed and said, "The surprise, Mamá. He wants the surprise!"

"Oh, he *does,* does he? Just a minute." She went into the back room and returned with several newspaper clippings and a book. She handed the clippings to Tomás and the book to Javier and said, "Maria got this for you. The book is about the *American Star.* Maria did some research and got this *libro* (lee'-bro). It should help you find out more about the ship. The clippings are from various Spanish newspapers that covered the wreck."

Javier's eyes became wide. He read the book's cover as best he could since it was written in English.

Señora Díaz said, "Maria says that the ship, *America,* is the wrecked *American Star.* There are pictures in this book of what the wrecked ship looked like a long time ago. It was expensive, but I had a little *dinero* (dee-neh-roh), put aside. I thought you both would enjoy looking at the pictures and maybe brushing up on your English, huh?"

"You mean you bought this book for us?" asked Tomás.

"*Sí,*" answered their mother. "Maria gets a discount, so she bought two of them. One for the store and one for us."

Tomás scooted his chair next to Javier's, and together they began to flip through the pages of the book.

"I was working over there a few days ago and she didn't say anything," declared Javier.

"Maria ordered it a few months ago. She can keep a secret, no?" She looked over her son's shoulders as they scanned the pages in the book. "See if you can find *American Star,* huh?"

Tomás looked over the newspaper articles while his brother buried himself in the book. As Tomás read one of the clippings, he saw the names that the *American Star* had been called during her long career. "Listen to this!" said Tomás. "The *American Star* has had *a lot* of names! This article lists them: *America,* USS *West Point, America, Australias, America, Italis, Noga, Alfredoss* and *American Star.*"

"Wow!" said Javier. "The old *hombre* I talked to said the ship had been owned many times! He wasn't kidding!" He quickly looked in the book for the name *America* in the table of contents. "Chapter Three," Javier announced. He turned to the page that began the chapter. One of the pages in this chapter had a picture of a woman in a nicely tailored dress and hat, holding a large bottle next to the hull of the ship.

Tomás leaned over his brother's shoulder to look at the picture. "Why is she doing that?" he asked.

"They christen ships just like *bebes,*" explained Javier. "That's how they get their names."

"So, that lady is the ship's godmother?" asked Tomás.

"I guess so," replied Javier.

"Who is she?" asked Tomás.

"Let me read it, and I can tell you," said Javier. "It says she was Señora Eleanor Roosevelt. She named the liner in 1939. Her husband was the thirty-second president of the *Estados Unidos.*"

Señora Díaz smiled at her two boys and shook her head as they continued to explore information about the ship.

"What is in the bottle?" asked Tomás.

"Champagne!" said Señora Díaz.

"Well, that's a waste!" said Tomás. "Why didn't they use *agua*? They sprinkled *agua* on me when I was christened—right, Mamá?"

Señora Díaz smiled at her young son.

On another page of the book, a picture showed the stern section of the *America* when she was still under construction. Neatly written under the ship's name were the words "New York."

"How come that is written there?" asked Tomás leaning over his brother to get a better look.

Javier pushed his brother back into his own seat and said, "Do you mind?"

"I want to see!" explained Tomás.

"Me, too!" said Javier. "The city's name is written under the ship's name to tell where her home port is. Where she is registered."

"Oh!" exclaimed Tomás.

Javier turned the next few pages showing pictures of the *America* in several different shots. "Hold on a minute!" said Javier. He slipped from his chair and dashed upstairs to the loft. He came back down with the pictures he had taken of the wreck sight. He sat down and spread his pictures in front of him.

"What did you get those photos for?" asked Tomás.

"To compare what she looked like new and what she looks like now," explained Javier. He turned another page as they all looked at the pictures of the ship. The next page left Javier with a lump in his throat. He gasped at a frontal bow shot of a new *America*. The picture was taken at close range from near the water level looking upward at the ship's prow.

Tomás cried, "Look at that. You took a photo almost like that!"

Javier placed the picture he had taken of the ship in a similar pose beside the one taken when she was new. "Look at her now," Javier said.

"It's just so sad," said Señora Díaz, who had moved closer to see the ship which had besotted her boys.

The trio continued looking through the book, poring over more and more photographs. They saw officers in uniforms helping passengers, officers on the bridge during a voyage at sea, well-dressed passengers in suits or mink coats.

Tomás pointed to the engine telegraph in one picture and said, "Look! We saw that! Well—what is left of it."

Javier hesitated when a picture showed the first-class restaurant on the *America*. "We stood in this room, too," he said, slowly remembering the mysterious voices and sounds.

"*Sí*," said Tomás. "She sure doesn't look the same now."

"Hmm!" said their mother. "You show me a photo of any *señora* taken fifty years ago and you'll see that none of them look the same! It goes with living! We all age. Nothing stays the same."

"But a *transatlántico* isn't really a living thing. Is it?" asked Tomás.

"Yes it is," exclaimed Javier. "Ships are planned, constructed, taken care of, repaired— They are a lot like people. They all have different temperaments, personalities. Remember, dwarf, they even get christened," he said, nudging his brother.

"Like us—right, Mamá?" said Tomás.

"*Sí*," stated their mother.

There were pictures of the ship at sea in bad storms, docking in various ports of call. There were even pictures of what the ship looked like in other colors and names.

Tomás pointed to a picture of the ship as the *Italis* and said, "That's when she lost her other funnel. I like her better with two smokestacks and her hull painted black, the top part white, and the smokestacks colored red, white and blue."

"Me, too," agreed Javier. Javier turned the pages to the second chapter. In this chapter, there was a picture of a man sitting atop a ventilator with a red, white, and blue smokestack in the background. He seemed to be an important man. As Javier gazed over the picture, his eyes came to rest on the man's face, which looked very familiar to him. The man was immaculately dressed, and in every picture he wore a tie, an old battered hat and wire-rimmed glasses. Javier held the book closer. "It can't be!" he exclaimed.

"What is it?" asked his mother.

"This *hombre*! This man in the photo! He looks just like the fellow I met at Playa de Garcey! He is the one who has been telling me about the ship. This can't be!" cried Javier.

"Well," Mamá said. "The *libro* is new."

"Maybe that *is* him," argued Tomás.

"This photo was taken in the 1940s, Tomás!" yelled Javier. "Look at him then!"

Tomás looked at his mother and shrugged while Javier still clung to the book.

Señora Díaz looked at Javier and said, "There are a lot of God's people who look similar. He probably just looks like him. No?"

"Only if they're twins!" said Javier.

"Maybe he is a relative or something!" said his mother.

"If this *is* the same person, he is over one hundred years old!" exclaimed Javier.

"You boys look at the book. I will get dinner started," said their mother, chuckling to herself. "What nonsense!"

"I have to work on my English translations," confessed Javier. "I will try and figure out what this book says. I have got to find out about this *gringo*."

62

"Me, too!" chimed in Tomás, smiling.

"Okay, dwarf," said Javier. Together the boys began to read the book.

After dinner, Javier and Tomás climbed into their beds, and Javier continued reading the book aloud to his brother. As Javier read, the story of the mysterious *American Star* began to piece itself together into a life filled with history and happiness.

Study Questions for Chapter Six

1. Explain what is meant by "mournful echo" on page 47.
2. Javier had two flashbacks when he went aboard the ship. Compare and contrast how these experiences were both alike and different.
3. What is a corridor?
4. On page 56, Señora Díaz states she doesn't want her children telling her "half-truths"; explain why she said this and the conversation she had with her sons about half-truths.
5. Javier and Tomás read about the ship and discovered a number of interesting facts. Name three facts that they learned about the ship from their research.
6. Make a prediction about who you think the old man in the story is. How did you come to your conclusion?

Activity:

1. With a parent or teacher's permission, log on to the Web site *www.gibbscox.com* and see what information you can find about designing ships and some of the ships that Gibbs and Cox have designed in the past.

Seven
Maritime History

"According to the book," said Javier, "the *American Star* was originally designed by an *hombre* named William Francis Gibbs. William Francis Gibbs was a naval architect who, along with his brother Frederick, started the company of Gibbs and Cox in New York, in the United States."

"Maybe you saw his *hermano* (air-mah'-noh)," suggested Tomás.

"His brother doesn't wear the hat, William Francis does. Quiet, dwarf!" commanded Javier, as he continued reading. "Señor Gibbs graduated from law school and also received a graduate degree in accounting. He designed several ships before designing the *America*. The *America* was built in the *Estates Undoes*. President Roosevelt's wife christened the liner on August 31, 1939, the day before Adolf Hitler invaded Poland, launching the Second World War," concluded Javier.

"Wow!" exclaimed Tomás. "We studied about Hitler in *escuela*. He's that guy with the little black mustache who put Jews in concentration camps. He was mean. He wanted to rule Europe."

"He wanted to rule the world!" corrected Javier. "I lost my place," he said, scanning the page. "The *America* was operated by the United States Lines Company. She briefly acted as a luxury liner and then was taken over by the Navy to act as an auxiliary vessel during World War II. She was renamed the USS *West Point* during her war career. Hey! That explains those chunks of gray paint we saw on her hull where it had broken. She was a troop transport. She was a gray ghost then and is a blue ghost now." Javier continued to read. "The USS *West Point* could carry 8,000 troops at a time between America and Europe. She outran several enemy ships, and she usually sailed alone. She had limited maintenance, but she never had a breakdown at sea. After her time in the Navy, she was reclaimed by her owners and again became the *America*. In 1952, the *America* was given a sister *transatlántico* as a running mate on the Atlantic. Her sister was bigger, longer, and faster and was Señor Gibbs's dream come true. This ship's name was *United States*. The *America* was overshadowed by her.

"I was just thinking, that old man on the *playa* said that he had neglected the ship. He said that she was always self-reliant, and that he never had to worry about her," said Javier. "He knows so much about her. Things that only an expert could know."

"Is he worried about her now?" questioned Tomás.

"*Sí*," said Javier. "Let's keep on reading. In 1964, Chandris Lines, a Greek shipping company, bought the *America* from the United States Lines. The new owners named her the *Australias*."

"What does Australias mean?" asked Tomás.

"Australian lady," answered Javier.

"She is a lady," confirmed Tomás.

"The *Australias* sailed from Australia and New Zealand to Europe and other destinations. She was repainted all white with aqua blue on her funnels. Two large X's were attached to the funnels, symbols of the Chandris Lines."

"How come they were X's and not C's?" asked Tomás.

"Because they're Greek. In 1978, Chandris sold the *Australias* to a new American company named Ventura Cruises. She was again named the *America*. The company declared bankruptcy and the neglected *America* was put up for auction. Chandris repurchased the ship and restyled her with one funnel and named her *Italis*. From the *Italis* she was sold and became the *Noga* and then she became the *Alferdoss*. I guess we know what happened after that."

The boys continued to read until their mother made them stop for the night and go to bed.

"Lights out, you two!" called their mother from downstairs.

Javier could not get the ship out of his mind. During the night, he had strange dreams about her. He kept hearing the sound of the ocean and a distant foghorn calling out to him. He saw the old man dressed all in white and the dark spaniel, Chota, alongside him, walking on the deck of the ship.

The next day, after school, Javier drove to the wreck site by himself. When he pulled up to the beach, he saw that there were several emergency vehicles parked there. Looking further out toward the wreck itself, Javier could see a group of people in the water and some rescue boats nearby. He got out of the Jeep and walked down to the surf, watching the activity. As he stood there, he was suddenly aware that the old man was standing beside him. He looked over and said, "What is going on out there?"

"Another drowning," answered the old man.

"What do you mean, another?" questioned Javier.

"There have been several people who have drowned

going out to the ship," said the old man shaking his head. "Foolishness!"

"You said that this would happen," remembered Javier.

"Yes, I did," said the old man. "I am glad that you listened to me and that you were cautious."

"*Sí*, I am, too," agreed Javier. He looked at the old man's face as he stood beside him staring out to sea. The man noticed Javier watching him intently.

"Forgive me, *señor*, for staring. It is just that you look so much like someone's photo I saw recently."

The old man smiled and gave Javier an understanding nod.

"I have been reading about the *American Star* in this book that my mother bought for me," explained Javier. "The book is really great! It tells about the ship's history. It's really cool."

The old man's eyes lit up.

Javier continued, "The book has the *America* in it. That was the ship's original name when it was first launched. Anyway, after reading about it, I understand now what you meant about the ship not going without a fight and how much she has meant to people. I suppose any one of the thousands she transported home during the war was very grateful for her. Of course, that doesn't even touch those who have sailed on her for pleasure through the years. According to the book, the *American Star* is over fifty-four years old. That's really old for a ship."

The old man watched Javier with amusement. "Yes, it is," he replied. "So there is finally a book that has been written about the ship. Well, imagine that; after all these years."

"*Sí*," responded Javier as he watched the rescue

team. "There are a lot of accounts about the ship." The old man looked questioningly at him. "I work at a little bookstore in town. The owner ordered the book for me." The old man nodded in understanding yet remained silent.

The two of them stood quietly watching the rescue team. Finally, Javier spoke, "I probably would have tried swimming out to the wreck, too, if you hadn't warned me about the bad sea currents," he admitted. "Did you warn any others?"

"It is best to invest your time wisely with people who are intuitive and open-minded," said the old man.

"I wish there was something I could do to help all of them," said Javier. "But I would just be in the way."

"Your time to help someone is coming soon," said the old man.

"What?" questioned Javier.

"There is nothing you can do for that poor soul," said the old man, nodding toward the drowned victim. "That man, just like several others, has chosen his own fate."

"Do you think he'll really die?" asked Javier.

The old man shook his head sadly and said, "I'm sorry to say he's already gone."

Javier crossed himself, pulled the rosary beads from his pocket, closed his eyes, and lowered his head in prayer.

After some time had passed, the old man said, "Your prayers are in earnest."

"I hope they are answered," said Javier. "Since I can't save his life, I can at least pray for his soul." Javier placed the beads back inside his jean's pocket. "Why do things like this have to happen?" he asked. "Why don't people think?"

"Arrogance," answered the old man.

Study Questions for Chapter Seven

1. Who was the naval architect who designed the SS *America?*
2. Compare/contrast the SS *America* to the aircraft carrier USS *Ronald Reagan.*
3. Do some research about World War II and explain why the United States declared war on the Japanese.
4. What was happening in Europe when the *America* went to sea? How would this impact the ship later?
5. Using the timeline chart below, label the life and events of the SS *America* from 1939 to 1994.

1939   1994

/--/-------/--------------------/-----------/--/----------/-------------/------------------/

6. How did the SS *America* help the United States Navy during World War II?

Eight
Rescue

Javier and Tomás sat in the living room completing their homework. They listened to the gentle falling rain on the roof. As the boys studied, a knock was heard on the front door. Before the boys could put down their books to see who was outside, Carlos bound into the room.

"Hey!" called Carlos, as he entered the house.

"Come on in," said Javier.

"Who is it, Javier?" called Señora Díaz from the kitchen.

"It's Carlos," called Javier.

"*Hola,* Carlos! Wipe your feet!" called Señora Díaz.

Carlos looked at Javier and laughed. He followed Señora Díaz's orders, took off his rain jacket and placed it on a rack by the front door.

"What's up?" asked Javier.

"Other than putting pots and pans all over our *casa* to catch rainwater seeping through the damaged roof, nothing," said Carlos as he sat on the couch.

"Your stepdad still hasn't gotten enough lumber to finish the job on the roof, has he?" said Javier.

"No, he hasn't," said Carlos, sighing. "I have tried to help him out with the little *dinero* I make at the orchards, but it isn't enough. Anyway, the reason I stopped by was to see if I could get you to help me move something."

"Sure!" said Javier agreeably.

"Well, you might want to wait and answer me after you hear what it is," he warned.

Javier looked long and suspiciously at his friend and said, "What?" Carlos took a deep breath and said, "I have found a real good thing to get off the ship. I know how you feel about taking things from the wreck, but I have my reasons for wanting them. Anyway, I wanted to see if you would help me."

Javier looked hard at his friend with disbelief and said, "Carlos, you *know* how strongly I feel about people looting the liner! People like you are stripping her of her last shred of dignity. It's like taking the jewelry off a dead body while it's helplessly lying there. Or talking about what everyone's been left in a will while they stand around the dead guy's casket! Man! I don't believe you!"

"Just hear me out," interrupted Carlos.

"Do you even realize how dangerous it is to go out there?" interrupted Javier. "We went with a group of people to the wreck before, but for just the two of us to go out there with the currents getting worse is *loco*. I was at Playa de Garcey not long ago and watched a rescue team bag a body. A fellow had tried to swim out to the wreck and drowned! What could be so important that you are willing to risk your life? What if you fall climbing up the hull?"

"Javier, I have a plan."

"I don't want to hear it! You are taking something that doesn't belong to you! No way, man! No way!"

"I knew you wouldn't understand!" cried Carlos as he jumped to his feet. He looked over at Tomás, who was sitting very quietly watching the exchange. "Do you believe this guy? Don't you get to be as righteous and stubborn as your brother!" commanded Carlos. Tomás sat very still and didn't say a word. "Not everything in life is black or white, as you would have it, Javier! I thought that you were my *amigo*!" he yelled.

Javier rose to meet Carlos' eyes and replied, "I *am* your *amigo*! I care that you steal! I care that you would risk your life!"

"I am not stealing! I *have* to do this!" retorted Carlos. "It is about more than just *me*!"

"What is that supposed to mean?" questioned Javier, looking at him with suspicion. "Are you in some kind of trouble, Carlos?"

"No, nothing like what you are thinking!" he answered. "Some trust you have in me! All you do is judge other people! You even judged poor Saleena! Never mind! I was *loco* to think you would help me!" Carlos grabbed his jacket and left the house, slamming the door behind him.

Señora Díaz peeked around the corner from the kitchen and looked at Javier with raised eyebrows. "What was *that* about?" she asked.

"I am really not sure," said Javier, looking bewildered.

The next day, Javier noticed that Carlos was not in school. He and Tomás walked home alone. They got a snack and went upstairs to change into some old clothes to help Uncle Antonio with the goat farm when a pounding came on the back door of the kitchen. Javier and Tomás heard muffled voices, and then their mother poked her head in their room and said, "You boys are needed downstairs. Come quickly!"

Javier and Tomás looked at each other and bolted down the narrow stairs and burst into the kitchen. Carlos's mother, Señora Fuentes, was sitting at the kitchen table with a wild, troubled look in her eyes. It was evident that she was distraught and, from the smears on her cheeks, that she had been crying.

"Javier," said Señora Fuentes in a weak voice, "have you seen my Carlos today? Do you know where he is? I am *so* worried! I have been to several people's houses—nobody has seen him!" She began to sob again.

Señora Díaz put one hand on each of Señora Fuentes's shoulders and held her. She looked at her boys and said, "Señora Fuentes tells me that Carlos did not come home last night."

"He was not in *escuela* today either," said Javier. He shot a questioning look at his mother. She gave him a slight nod. "I do not know where Carlos is, Señora Fuentes, but I think that I can probably find him," said Javier. "Tomás and I will go look for him. We won't come back until we've found him."

Señora Díaz said, "Carlos's *mamá* will stay here with me while you boys go look for him." She gently hugged Señora Fuentes, who was still crying.

"Tomás and I will call you as soon as we can, Mamá," said Javier. "We will stop by and tell Uncle Antonio. He will go with us. I will then call my friend Miguel at the military base from Uncle Antonio's house and see if he can help us, too. Try not to worry Señora Fuentes."

Señora Díaz smiled sweetly at her son and rubbed her arms as if trying to keep herself warm in the 29° Celsius heat.

Tomás looked down at the floor where Tauben lay. "Come on, boy. You are coming, too!"

Tauben quickly rose and followed the boys out of the kitchen door. When they got outside, Javier looked gravely at Tomás and said, "You know where we are going, don't you?"

"*Sí,*" answered Tomás, "the *transatlántico.*"

"*Sí,*" answered Javier. "We will get Uncle Antonio and call Miguel and ask him to meet us on the *playa*. He can bring a boat for us to use to get out to the wreck."

"Okay!" said Tomás, hopping in the Jeep with Tauben.

The boys drove to Uncle Antonio's farm. They ran inside and, within minutes, Uncle Antonio came out of the house with the boys sprinting across the yard. They had blankets, flashlights, a first-aid kit and some bottled water. They placed everything in the Jeep and took off in hopes of finding Carlos.

The Jeep pulled up in the beachfront facing the wreck of the *American Star*. The sun was lowering itself in the sky, casting an eerie light through the superstructure, giving the appearance that she was illuminated from within. Uncle Antonio looked at the sun and then at his watch. Miguel came running up to them, dressed in his army fatigues and boots. "I have been waiting for you!" Miguel said. "What is this big emergency? Have you had second thoughts about Saleena?" he said teasingly.

"Miguel, this is serious! My friend, Carlos, hasn't been seen since last night and I have strong reason to believe he is on the wreck and may be in trouble! He came to our house last night, asking me to help him move something from the wreck. I told him that I wouldn't. We exchanged strong words with one another and he became angry and left. No one has seen him since. His *mamá* came to us this afternoon looking for him; otherwise, I wouldn't have known."

"Wow!" said Miguel. "You're right—this does look to be pretty serious. I will place a call to my company and put a helicopter on standby just in case we need to airlift Carlos out of the ship."

"Since you made sergeant, you've really got some pull, don't you?"

"The military doesn't usually bother with something of this nature, but we will do our best. I will also put a diving crew on alert. He may have gotten caught in the undertow if he swam out to the ship last night. Did he have a boat?"

"From here there looks like a raft is tied up near the ship's hull," said Javier.

"Are you sure he is on the wreck?" asked Miguel.

"Positive," stated Javier.

Miguel put his binoculars up to his eyes and scanned the wreck sight. "Do you know which piece of the wreck he was headed to?" asked Miguel.

"Not a clue," said Javier.

Miguel continued to scan the ship with his binoculars.

"Do you see *anything?*" asked Javier.

"Nothing," stated Miguel. "We better get started. It looks like we have a long night in front of us. I brought a boat to get us to the wreck site," he said. "It is a military boat with emergency supplies. I just hope that we don't need them."

Javier, Miguel and Uncle Antonio began walking toward the boat. Tomás ran after his brother, catching up to him, saying, "What am I supposed to do?"

"You stay here," commanded Javier.

Tomás opened his mouth to protest, but stopped. He saw the grave look on his brother's face.

"Somebody has to stay here on the beach in case we need more help. You have the most important job of all," said Javier. "If we are not back in three hours, go get more help."

Tomás cast a look at his uncle, who nodded in agreement. Javier threw Tomás the keys to the Jeep. "You have Tauben to keep you company," said Javier reassuringly. "There is a flashlight and binoculars in the Jeep, if you need them."

"But I don't know how to drive that well," cried Tomás. "I have only driven around our yard."

"You know enough to get help if you need it," said Javier calmly.

Tomás stood looking at his brother and slowly gave him a "thumbs-up" sign. Miguel, who had been talking to the military base, said, "Here, Tomás," as he threw him a walkie-talkie. "Listen to this in case I call you from the wreck. That way, you will know what's going on." Tomás nodded to Miguel while he studied the walkie-talkie. Miguel continued to talk to the base on his radio as he walked to the rescue boat. Tomás watched with anxiousness as his brother, uncle, and Miguel pushed the boat out and headed toward the wreck. Tomás walked over and rummaged in the Jeep, finding the binoculars. He used them to watch the trio as they made their way toward the dimly outlined *American Star*.

As Tomás sat in the Jeep with Tauben, he watched the sun sink lower in the sky. "The stars will be out soon," he said. The dog lay on the backrest with his head on his forepaws, his tail wagging gently.

Tomás was aware that he was no longer alone on the beach. He turned to see a man dressed all in white standing beside the Jeep. Tauben sat on the backrest and continued to wag his tail. The man smiled at Tomás. As Tomás looked at the man's face, he suddenly realized that the face was familiar to him. Tomás couldn't place where he had seen him before. Nevertheless, he had some faint recollection of it.

The old man said, "Are you stargazing tonight?"

"I am keeping watch on the *American Star,*" he answered. "My brother's friend, Carlos, is on the ship and we are afraid he's been hurt."

The old man cast a protective eye on the ship and then looked back at Tomás and said, "Your brother is alone?"

"Oh, no, *señor*. My uncle and his friend, Miguel, are with him."

"I see," said the old man.

"Do they know where Carlos is?" inquired the old man.

"No, *señor,*" replied Tomás. "That's the problem. He could be anywhere."

"I see. They need some guidance."

Tomás turned around to pet Tauben and said, "*Sí.*" When he looked back, the old man was gone. Tomás felt a warm breeze from the sea. On the horizon, the first bright star appeared in the sky as the night's veil began to descend. Tomás sat stroking Tauben's head, watching the starlight become increasingly brighter as the outlined superstructure of the ship continued to fade with the setting sun.

The rescue party approached the shipwreck. As they drew nearer, Miguel held the binoculars to his eyes. He had a worried look on his face. "What do you see?" questioned Javier. Miguel handed the binoculars to Javier and nodded in the direction of the stern. Javier held the binoculars up to his eyes. Since it was getting dark, it was difficult to see, but he strained hard to focus and he said, "Oh, my gosh!"

"What is it?" asked Uncle Antonio.

Miguel said, "There is a thin stream of smoke coming from windows on the Promenade Deck closest to the bow."

Uncle Antonio's eyebrows narrowed, and he gazed in

the general direction of the ship. He turned to Miguel and said, "This could be a break."

As the rescue party approached the bow section of the wreck, they tied their boat to the hull and climbed the ladder. The smoke was becoming more intense. Miguel lugged the small fire extinguisher from the boat up the ladder with him. The Promenade windows were right by the ladder and were filling with smoke. However, the source of the smoke was coming from farther inside the deck.

As Javier climbed the ladder, he said aloud, "This is *loco*! Why Carlos wanted something from this wreck is beyond me!"

Uncle Antonio responded by saying, "You really don't have any idea why he would do this?"

"No!" yelled Javier in exasperation.

"Perhaps he has a reason that you do not know about," said Uncle Antonio reaching for the next rung of the ladder.

"It better be good, whatever the reason," hissed Javier through clenched teeth. He struggled to gain sure footing on each rung of the ladder while holding onto the blanket and flashlight he was carrying. Uncle Antonio had the first-aid kit and some bottled water.

Nearing the Promenade Deck windows, the thickening smoke continued to pour out. Miguel reached the windows first and quickly dropped the fire extinguisher onto the deck of the Promenade. He hoisted himself inside and searched in his pocket for a bandana to hold over his nose as he dropped to the ship's deck. The smoke was intense. It stung his eyes and burned his throat. The source of the fire was found inside the lobby next to the starboard elevator. He sprayed the fire extinguisher's foam on the fire and the smoke began to dissipate. He rose from the deck and continued dowsing the small fire. Javier and Uncle Antonio hauled themselves aboard the wreck behind Miguel. Miguel stood over a smoldering pile of sheets, curtains, mattresses, and towels dowsing them with what was left of the extinguisher's foam. Javier shielded his eyes and mouth with a bandana while fanning smoke away with his one free arm.

"I think I know what caused this," said Uncle Antonio, kicking a charred lantern away from the smoldering debris. "What was Carlos thinking, leaving a lighted lantern close to flammable materials?"

"That is the million-dollar question," said Javier, wiping tears away from his dark eyes. "He should know better than that."

"This is under control," stated Miguel. "Let's go look for Carlos."

"I don't know where to begin," coughed Javier.

"Time is wasting," said Uncle Antonio looking at his watch. He motioned for Javier and Miguel to follow him. They walked through the smoking room, which had a circular shape. They called out Carlos's name as they walked through the dark ship. They each held a flashlight and used the penetrating beams to guide their steps as they walked through. The haunting echo of Carlos's name in the dismal ship sent chills down Javier's back. Occasionally they would stop and listen in hopes of hearing a response to their calls, but there was none. The group moved toward the main lounge. Entering this part of the ship, the group heard what sounded like a barking dog. Javier, Miguel, and Uncle Antonio looked at each other in the darkness and began to follow the dog's bark.

"Am I going *loco* or did you all hear a dog barking?" inquired Uncle Antonio.

"No, you are not *loco*. We heard it, too," confirmed Miguel.

"What would a dog be doing on this shipwreck?" asked Javier as they continued to follow its voice. The barking led them into the main lounge. Javier shone his flashlight on something that appeared to be at the end of the room. At first, he thought it was just a piece of furniture, but then it moved.

"What is it?" asked Uncle Antonio.

"I don't know," answered Javier.

The object again moved and then barked. Javier immediately cast a beam of light on it. There, sitting beside a jumble of doors on the deck was a dark cocker spaniel. The dog nervously stamped its forepaws on the deck and whined.

"Chota?" said Javier inching closer.

The dog barked again and whined.

"You recognize this *perro*?" asked Uncle Antonio.

"*Sí*, he was with the old man I talked to on the beach," said Javier.

"What is it doing on this wreck?" asked Miguel.

"I don't know," answered Javier. "But he is definitely trying to tell us something!"

The group inched their way closer to the dog as the flashlight's beam illuminated the area revealing two massive doors lying askew on a mound. The doors were made of mahogany wood, bronze, and had Art Deco-stenciled designs on the frosted glass inserts.

"These are the doors to the lounge," announced Javier. "Those doors weren't like that when we were here last." The doors had been taken from their hinges. Javier shined his flashlight over the tumbled doors, and sticking out from underneath one of the doors was a pair of sneakers.

"Carlos!" yelled Javier.

As Javier and Miguel peeled the doors from Carlos, they saw that he was unconscious and bleeding from his temple. His right arm was bruised and swollen. Uncle Antonio knelt down and quickly felt his neck for a pulse.

"Is he breathing?" questioned Javier.

"He is alive," said Uncle Antonio. "He has a pulse."

Uncle Antonio knelt over Carlos and listened to his lungs. He watched to see if they rose and fell. Uncle Antonio wet his forefinger and stuck it under Carlos's nose. He could feel the warm air coming from it as he exhaled. Uncle Antonio looked up at Javier and Miguel's anxious faces and said, "He is breathing." Javier and Miguel sighed with relief. Uncle Antonio opened his first-aid kit and looked for an ammonia swab. He unwrapped it and gently placed it under Carlos's nose to bring him to consciousness. Miguel opened the bottled water and began pouring it on a clean bandana.

Javier dropped to his knees and bowed his head in prayer. Miguel handed the damp bandana to Uncle Antonio and then radioed the military base, asking for medical help. He requested a helicopter to come and airlift Carlos from the wreck.

Tomás sat in the Jeep on shore and heard Miguel's transmission to the base. He tightened his already firm grip on Tauben's neck. "I'm scared," he whispered into his dog's ear.

"We have got to get him to an open deck," said Miguel.

Uncle Antonio looked around the empty room. "We need something to transport him onto the open decks."

Carlos began to move his head a little. He grunted in pain.

"He is beginning to come to," said Uncle Antonio. He

fiddled with some bottles in the first-aid kit and began to wipe the blood from Carlos's head with the clean, damp bandana.

Javier leaned down to his friend's ear and said, "Carlos, it is me—Javier. Don't move. We are going to get you out of here. Don't worry. Everything is going to be fine."

Carlos's eyelids fluttered and then opened. His eyes frantically searched the faces staring down at him. He tried to move his arm and then groaned with pain.

Uncle Antonio said, "Carlos, do you know where you are?"

Carlos gently nodded his head yes.

Uncle Antonio said, "Can you speak?"

Carlos softly answered, "I—think—so."

Javier, Uncle Antonio, and Miguel looked at each other with relief.

Javier said, "Carlos, where are you?"

Carlos faintly said, "The *transatlántico*."

"That's right! You are on the *American Star*. Man, I am *so angry* at you for going off without telling anyone where you were going. Do you know how scared we have all been? I tried to tell you not to come on this wreck, but you would not listen to me!" cried Javier.

Carlos closed his eyes and shook his head slowly at his friend. He tried to raise his arm again and winced in pain. This time, tears came to his eyes. Carlos said in a hoarse voice, "You . . . don't . . . understand . . . I . . . was . . . getting . . . these . . . doors . . . so that I . . . could sell them . . . to pay for . . . a new . . . roof for . . . our . . . *casa*."

"What?" exclaimed Javier.

Uncle Antonio shot a concerned look at Miguel, and they both came nearer to Carlos. Javier looked at his friend's swelling face and he went pale. "You did this because of the roof on your house?"

Carlos gently nodded his head. He continued, "I met an . . . *hombre* over at the . . . town of . . . Correlejo. He is a . . . tourist. He . . . was looking for . . . something . . . from the ship . . . for his club . . . in Lisbon. I told him . . . about the . . . doors. He said . . . he would . . . pay me well for them. . . . It was . . . the only way!"

Javier looked over at his uncle and Miguel. Javier said to them, "He asked me to come with him, but I told him no. This is all my fault." Javier hung his head in shame.

Uncle Antonio shook his head at Javier and said, "Javier, Carlos didn't tell you *why* he wanted to get something from the ship. Regardless of whether you had warned him or not, he made a choice. However, now you can see that his choice was not for selfish gain."

Javier looked at Carlos, "How did you ever think you could move those doors by yourself? Are you *loco*?"

The walkie-talkie blurted out with static voices, breaking the tension in the room. The base was confirming Miguel's position and his request for help. Miguel turned to Javier and said, "I am sure Tomás heard the radio call from the base. Hopefully he understands what is going on. It is a good thing we keep extra transmitters in our equipment belts." Miguel smiled as he held up his radio. "The base is sending a helicopter. We will take Carlos to one of the mainland hospitals."

"What . . . about . . . the . . . doors?" asked Carlos with difficulty. "If I don't get the . . . doors to . . . Correlejo by tomorrow . . . we will not . . . get the . . . roof."

Uncle Antonio patted Carlos's forehead and said, "Don't you worry, Carlos, Javier and I will get the doors out of here for you."

Javier gently spoke to Carlos and said, "I am *so sorry* that I told you no. It is just that I don't like taking something that belongs to someone else."

Carlos said, "I . . . know you don't. But . . . my family . . . is more . . . important . . . to me than . . . rules."

Javier looked at his friend, and a dawn of realization came over him. He said, "We have been through a lot together. I won't let you down. I will get the doors and take them to Correlejo with Uncle. You will get that new roof, Carlos. I promise."

Carlos smiled faintly and said, "*Gracias, amigo.*"

Uncle Antonio continued to bandage Carlos's head as Miguel went in search of a flat board on which to transport him. Uncle Antonio said, "Carlos, I just remembered, your lantern turned over and caught some materials on fire there off the Promenade Deck. If it weren't for the smoke coming from this part of the wreck, we wouldn't have known where you were."

Carlos looked at Uncle Antonio. "Lantern?" he asked hoarsely. "I . . . had no . . . lantern. I . . . brought . . . my flashlight. It . . . is . . . over there." Carlos tossed his throbbing head in the direction of the door frame where the doors had hung. Carlos's large flashlight lay on the floor. Javier looked at his uncle. Uncle Antonio asked, "Do you know if anyone else has been on the wreck today?"

"I . . . guess . . . I . . . have . . . been . . . out . . . for a while," replied Carlos. "I . . . do . . . not . . . know."

"The lantern seems to be as much of a mystery as the dog," said Uncle Antonio.

"What dog?" asked Carlos looking startled.

"A cocker spaniel," answered Uncle Antonio. "He led us through the ship to where you were."

"Are you . . . sure . . . that you all . . . didn't get . . . hit in the . . . head, too?" said Carlos.

"We definitely saw the dog. It looked like Chota Peg," said Javier, smiling.

"What would that dog be doing on this wreck? Unless he was brought aboard by someone!" stated Uncle Antonio.

"Where is . . . the dog now?" asked Carlos hoarsely.

"I don't know," said Javier. "He was here."

"Well, he isn't here now," stated Uncle Antonio.

"There . . . was no . . . dog on . . . this wreck when . . . I came . . . aboard," said Carlos.

"Well, he came aboard sometime," insisted Javier. "Unless of course if he was—" Javier's voice trailed off and he suddenly turned pale.

"What is it?" asked Uncle Antonio with concern.

"I read about a dog named Chota Peg in that book. The dog was raised on—"

"On what?" asked Uncle Antonio.

"On this ship—I mean, the *America*," answered Javier faintly. "Chota was Captain John Anderson's dog, and he had lived on the ship since he was a pup. He was so used to the ship that he even rode the elevators! And that's where we found him, by the elevator!"

"*Now* who's *loco*?" jeered Uncle Antonio.

The group suddenly heard an approaching helicopter. Miguel came back into the lounge carrying a flatboard, and with Uncle Antonio's help they began to maneuver Carlos onto it.

Miguel said to Javier, "If you go back the way we came in here and head aft on the Promenade Deck, you will come to steps that will lead up two decks; then top side onto the deck near the funnel. The helicopter will see you from there. I will take all of these flashlights so they can see us," he said, tossing his head in the direction of the flashlights lying on the floor. "Hurry up."

Uncle Antonio lifted Carlos onto the board. As Javier gathered up his things, he noticed a set of discarded stateroom keys lying on the deck. He picked them up and put them into his pants pocket. Then the group slowly began to walk Carlos through the ship. After maneuvering through dark corridors with the aid of minimal light, they reached the outer decks near the funnel. The military helicopter hovered close to the wreck. Miguel directed it with the two flashlight beams. The helicopter did not land, for fear that the extra weight of the aircraft would cause the ship to list further or possibly collapse the decks altogether. The helicopter crew lowered a basket down to the deck while Uncle Antonio waited for the harness to touch the ship, grounding the static electricity created by the helicopter's whirling blades. Then Carlos was loaded into the basket and lifted by the helicopter.

Tomás stood on the beach with Tauben, watching the lights of the helicopter and listening to the sounds of its massive blades. He watched as the helicopter moved away from the wreck and disappeared into the darkness of the night. After what seemed an eternity, three flashlight beams penetrated the night as the trio made their way down the side of the ship's hull. It wasn't long until they were back on shore. Tomás ran down to meet the boat. Javier and Miguel pulled the boat onto the shore, while Uncle Antonio gathered his gear.

"Is Carlos going to be all right?" asked Tomás.

"Sí," answered Miguel as he wound the boat's rope around his arm. "He was hurt, but he will be okay."

"I was getting really worried about you guys. Then, I heard your radio call to the base," said Tomás. "I saw the helicopter coming and everything! I guess the old man guided you like he said he would."

"The old man?" asked Javier.

"The old *hombre* who talked to me on the beach. He talked to me just after you set off for the wreck," answered Tomás.

"What did he look like?" asked Javier.

"I don't know. He was old and he wore glasses."

"What else was he wearing?"

"He was dressed all in white and wore an old battered hat," said Tomás.

"Did he look like the old man I showed you from the book?" asked Javier.

Tomás thought for a moment and said, "Yeah. I guess in a way he did."

Javier looked at Miguel with a wistful smile. Miguel said, "We didn't see any old man on the ship."

"No," corrected Javier, "but we saw a dog. That dog belongs to a friend of the old man, and it's always with him."

"I told the *hombre* what had happened to Carlos and that you all were going out to the wreck to look for him," said Tomás.

"When was this?" asked Uncle Antonio.

"A while after you left. It was still light," answered Tomás. "He petted Tauben. It was as if Tauben knew him. He didn't growl or anything."

"We don't have time to stand here and go over this," said Uncle Antonio. "We've got to get back and let Carlos's *mamá* know that he's all right. We also have to take her over to the hospital."

"Uncle Antonio, you take the Jeep and get Señora Fuentes. Tomás and I will get a ride with Miguel."

"Okay," confirmed Uncle Antonio. He climbed into the Jeep and drove off to inform Señora Fuentes what had happened to Carlos and where he had been taken. The boys watched as the lights from the Jeep disappeared.

Miguel said, "I don't know about either of you, but I am starving! I will run up to the base and see what I can find to tide us over! I will be back with food and wheels."

"Thanks, Miguel," called Javier to his friend. "I don't know what we would have done without your help tonight. I don't know what to do to make it up to you."

"No problem," said Miguel, smiling. "You repay my kindness by talking to Saleena. You take her out again, huh?"

Javier shook his head at his friend and said, "You have me there."

Miguel scampered up the beach in search of something for the boys to eat.

"I am going to take Tauben down the beach for a run," announced Tomás. "He and I have both been sitting in the Jeep for a long time."

"Hey," said Javier. "I have something for you from the *transatlántico*," he said, tossing the keys to Tomás. "You have the keys to the ship. Don't drive recklessly."

Tomás studied the keys he had caught in his hand. "These are the keys to the ship?"

"They're a set of room keys."

"I thought we weren't to take anything from her?"

"I know," said Javier. "But those keys can't be used anymore and I thought you deserved something for being so brave tonight."

"GEE!! Thanks, Javier! WOW!!"

"Go on and take Tauben for a walk," directed Javier. "Be careful and don't go off anywhere!"

"I won't," promised Tomás, running down into the surf with Tauben. Javier stayed on the beach waiting for Miguel to return from the base. He sat down on the beach and gazed at the ship. A full moon was suspended in the night sky and it cast shadows on the beach and water. He envisioned the ship as she was when first at sea sailing the Atlantic as the SS *America*. He thought of her sleek black hull, white superstructure and her red, white, and blue funnels—trademarks of the United States Lines. What a beauty she had been. Suddenly, Javier's stomach rumbled, bringing him back from his dream. He sighed and said to himself, "I hope Miguel finds something to eat."

"You had a different kind of sustenance tonight," said a familiar voice. Javier looked up to see the old man's face staring down at him. Chota Peg was beside him.

Javier's eyes rested on the dog and he said, "Hey, Chota." The dog sat down beside the old man and looked at Javier. Javier rose to his feet and stared at the old man's face. After several moments he said, "*Gracias* for helping my friend."

The old man looked at Javier and said, "*You* were responsible for helping your friend."

"If it weren't for me, he might never have gotten hurt in the first place," stated Javier. "He came to me for help last night and I told him no. If I had helped him, this would never have happened!"

"You told Carlos how you felt about taking things from the ship," stated the old man.

"How did you know that?" asked Javier.

"Am I wrong?"

"No, sir," confirmed Javier.

"There is nothing wrong for standing up for what you believe to be right."

Javier was taken aback by the old man's frankness. He was silent for a while. "I did not know why Carlos wanted something from the ship. But I learned something tonight."

"And what might that be?" asked the old man.

91

"I only saw one side of what Carlos was asking of me. I saw *my* side. I did not stop to think that there could be another."

"And there was *another* side?" asked the old man.

"*Sí*," answered Javier.

"The world is filled with moral and ethical dilemmas, my boy. Most things are never black or white; they are gray—a mixture. When we are faced with these challenges, we must study all sides. You see, you learned a valuable lesson tonight. No matter how much some *thing* matters, some *one* matters more. Carlos wasn't looting the ship for profit; all he wanted was a sturdy roof over his family's head. He did the only thing he could see to do to help the others he loves. There is a difference! Wanting something—just to have it; or needing something."

"I understand," said Javier.

"Everyone deserves to be understood and perhaps to have a second chance," said the old man.

Javier looked out to sea. The wind tossed his coal-black hair. His good looks were outlined by the moon's bright light.

"You are thinking of something?" asked the old man.

"Someone," answered Javier. "Saleena. I did the same thing to her that I did to Carlos. I didn't stop to see her side, only mine."

"Ah," said the old man nodding his head slightly.

They both stood in the moon's light staring at the wreck of the *American Star*. Finally, Javier said, "Ships deserve second chances, too."

"How do you mean?" questioned the old man.

"The *American Star*," said Javier nodding toward the ship. "She was going to get a second chance being towed to Thailand. Instead, her second chance was taken away from her. This is where she ends. It is hard to understand why some people get a second chance, like Carlos, and others don't."

"Like your father?" questioned the old man.

Javier nodded silently.

"People live or die because it is allowed by a higher power. Not so with things such as ships," said the old man. "What is even worse, is a parent watching the destruction of their child and knowing there is nothing they can do about it. Carlos's mother knows that he will be all right by now," said the old man.

"What about you?" asked Javier.

"Me?" questioned the old man. "I don't follow."

"The planning, designing, overseeing, maintenance, smooth voyages, you know—It's hard when it all comes to an end. In a way, *you* seem to be the *American Star*'s parent. People make *transatlánticos,* but the *transatlánticos* themselves are only as important as the people who create them, crew them, and sail in them."

The old man smiled sweetly. He looked out across the sea. Javier wasn't sure, but he thought he detected a small tear in the old man's eye. The pair stood on the beach for a while as the moon bathed them in light. The dark outline of the broken and battered ship stood majestically in the distance.

Javier finally spoke, "Yes, you are her proud parent, *señor.* In life, as in death, you watch over her; just as God watches over us."

The old man looked down at Chota Peg, gently stroked his head and said, "Our work here is finished, boy." He turned to Javier with a twinkle in his eye and said, "And to think—I studied law!"

Javier watched as the man and dog walked down the beach and disappeared into the moon's lunar brilliance.

Study Questions for Chapter Eight

1. What is your opinion of what happened in this chapter between Carlos and Javier?
2. Do you think it was wrong of Javier to judge Carlos? Why or why not? Support your answer with facts from the text.
3. On page 79, what does it mean, "—the night's veil began to descend?"
4. There were several mysterious happenings on the shipwreck when they went to rescue Carlos. Why do you suppose these things occurred?
5. How was Carlos going to use the doors to help his family?
6. What is the author's purpose for writing this book?

Activity:

1. On the map at the right, label the places (in order) the ship passed on her last "voyage": Greece, Canary Islands, Spain, Straits of Gibraltar, Italy, Portugal, Morocco.

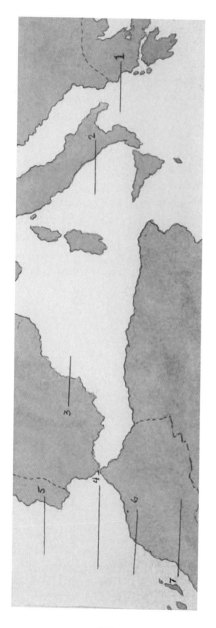

95

Epilogue

There have been several captains at the helm of the former SS *America* during her career on the oceans and seas of the world: Harry Manning, John Anderson, and Leroy Alexanderson, all of whom were with the United States Lines. William Francis Gibbs not only designed the SS *America* and her sister ship, the *United States*, but he designed Liberty ships and Victory ships during the Second World War as well. It is interesting to see the connections between the ships through both designer and ship's officers. Before his death, Alexanderson, last Commodore of the United States Lines fleet, was asked to sponsor the Victory ship, *American Victory,* when it opened as a floating museum in Tampa Bay, Florida in 2002.

The *American Victory* is a fifty-eight-year-old World War II era cargo ship that has been made into a passenger cruise vessel. The reconversion of the ship cost an estimated $3.5 million in donations and volunteers. The ship was first launched on June 20, 1945, and carried her first cargo to the Pacific two days after the Japanese surrendered. The ship continued to operate until she was retired and made part of the James River Reserve Fleet in Virginia, from 1985 until 1999. In 1999, the ship was restored by the nonprofit organization, American Victory Mariners Memorial and Museum. In 2002, the ship attracted an estimated 20,000 visitors.

ONE BROADWAY

NEW YORK

July 27, 1966

Dear Commodore Alexanderson:

This will confirm my telephone conversation today congratulating you on your elevation to Commodore of the United States Lines Fleet, effective July 29, 1966.

I doubt that it is possible for any other member of your organization to have a finer record than yours. What a man!

May I also add how much I appreciate your enthusiasm and helpfulness to me during my frequent telephone calls to you while at sea.

I look forward to a continuation of the very fine relationship we have enjoyed with you over the years and send you every good wish for health, happiness and continued success in your new position.

Sincerely,

William Francis Gibbs

Commodore L. J. Alexanderson,
S.S. UNITED STATES,
Pier 86, North River,
New York, New York 10019.

Chota Peg aboard the ship.

Integrated Teaching Skills

I. Reading Sub skills:
  A. Main idea-Storm/supporting details:
    1. Chapter 1: Main idea=Storm/supporting details=no electricity, downed trees, damage, ship in trouble at sea.
    2. Chapter 2: Main idea=Clubhouse/supporting details=debris in yard, Tomás's reaction, rubbish pile, burning of debris, ship.
    3. Chapter 3: Main idea=Ship/supporting details=military base, beach, Miguel, danger.
    4. Chapter 4: Main idea=Ship/supporting details=beach, old man, military base, damage to ship.
    5. Chapter 5: Main idea=Ship/supporting details=looting, damage to ship, old man, Chota Peg, tide, flashbacks in time, time as an element, ship's names, guilt, history, sequencing of events, geographic locations.
    6. Chapter 6: Main idea=Ship/supporting details=mystery, flashbacks, interior of ship, fibbing to their mother, names of the ship, reading.
    7. Chapter 7: Main idea=Ship/supporting details=maritime history (ships' names), christening of *America,* drowning.
    8. Chapter 8: Main idea-moral/supporting details=lessons argument, Javier giving Tomás keys to Jeep/ship, rescue, mystery.
  B. Sequencing of events
    1. Which name of the ship is introduced first?
    2. Which name was used before USS *West Point?*

3. What happened after Javier met the old man on the beach?
4. By which name was the ship known at the end?
5. What name did the ship have after she was the *Australias?*
6. Where did Javier go after he heard the loud *boom* outside of the house?
7. The old man had warned Javier of danger before the drowning. What had he said to Javier?
8. What was the gradual lesson that Javier was to learn?

C. Compare/contrast:
   1. Tomás and Javier (How are they alike/different?)
   2. Javier and Carlos (How are they alike/different?)
   3. SS *America*/USS *West Point* (How are they alike/different?)
   4. SS *America*/SS *American Star* (How are they alike/different?)
   5. Javier and the old man (How are they alike/different?)

D. Cause/effect relationships:
   1. Because there was a storm, what were the results (effects)?
   2. Because Carlos didn't listen to Javier, what were the results (effects)?
   3. Because the electricity was off, what were the effects?
   4. So that Señora Díaz would not know that Tomás and Javier went to the ship, what did they do?

101

5. Since Javier didn't like people looting the ship, what did the boys do?

6. How did Señora Díaz get the boys to admit they had lied to her since she knew they had gone to the ship?

E. Author's purpose:

1. How does the author inform the reader about the ship?

2. Does the author entertain readers? How?

3. Are readers persuaded in any way while reading this book? In what way?

4. What descriptive words or ideas does the author use throughout the book about the ship?

5. Which descriptive words or ideas does the author use throughout the book about the characters?

6. Why do you think the author wrote this book?

F. Fiction/nonfiction:

1. Facts about the ship—nonfiction

2. Facts about the Canary Islands—nonfiction

3. Facts about William Francis Gibbs—nonfiction

4. Plot of book—historical fiction

5. Characters of book—some fiction/some nonfiction

6. Outcome of story—fiction/nonfiction

G. Figurative language:

1. pg. 1 ". . . howled continuously around Fuerteventura Island and buffeted the small house."

2. pg. 4 "shooting an electric finger to the earth."
3. pg. 11 "like a fallen giant."
4. pg. 16 "cast a protective eye."
5. pg. 25 "She seemed to struggle to keep some dignity from the elements that were trying so desperately to claim her."
6. pg. 25 "She looks like a lifeless sea creature."
7. pg. 35 "Man, that's like taking jewelry off a dead body."
8. pg. 48 "He felt as if he were suddenly a part of a magical transformation."
9. pg. 79 ". . . as the night's veil began to descend."

H. Context clues/vocabulary development
   1. pg. 2, unfazed
   2. pg. 2, gnawing
   3. pg. 5, mournful
   4. pg. 7, brimming
   5. pg. 10, downed
   6. pg. 14, salvageable
   7. pg. 16, hoisted
   8. pg. 24, aground
   9. pg. 25, dignity
   10. pg. 29, seaworthy
   11. pg. 41, submerge
   12. pg. 48, commingle
   13. pg. 50, telegraph
   14. pg. 69, arrogance

I. Predictions/drawing conclusions
   1. Why did Javier hear the voices in the main dining room and the bridge of the ship?

2. Who was the old man who befriended Javier?
3. How will Javier treat Carlos from now on?
4. Do you think that Javier will contact Saleena? Why or why not?

J. Biography/autobiography:

Biography: William Francis Gibbs was born in Philadelphia, Pennsylvania on August 24, 1886. At the age of three, William began drawing ships, and he continued drawing ships for the rest of his life. William Francis Gibbs had a younger brother named Frederick, with whom he was very close. The brothers were from an affluent family and were fortunate to cross the Atlantic Ocean on such opulent liners as the *Lusitania* and the *Mauretania*.

In 1910, William Francis Gibbs left Harvard with a certificate of completion but received no degree because he had not taken enough required courses. However, in June of 1919, Mr. Gibbs graduated from Columbia University with a degree in law and a Masters of Art.

In 1920, the Gibbs brothers began a naval architecture firm, which eventually became Gibbs and Cox, Inc. At this writing, the Gibbs company is still in operation. Many famous ships were produced from the drawing boards of this company, such as the *Leviathan*'s reconversion, the *America, United States, Malolo, Santa Rosa,* USS *Mahan, Fire Fighter* and *North Wind.* He also designed many Victory ships and Liberty ships during the Second World War.

Mr. Gibbs's name became synonymous with

HARVARD
Alumni Bulletin

October 25, 1952

The Designer of the liner "United States": See The Graduate

quality. He won numerous awards for his ship designs and the safety with which the ships were constructed. William Francis Gibbs had always wanted to produce an award-winning superliner, and with the building of the *United States,* he achieved that dream. On September 6, 1967, at the age of 81, Mr. Gibbs died.

Autobiography: My name is Elizabeth Fletcher and I was born on May 14, 1963. I was an only child, so my cat, Sam, and I were good buddies. My father is a retired dentist and my mother is a retired English teacher. I was born in Newport News, Virginia, but grew up in the southwestern part of Virginia.

As a small child, I can recall looking across Hampton Roads and seeing the famous red, white, and blue smokestacks of the *United States* ship. I was fascinated by the ship, and my mother would take me to the Mariners' Museum so that I could learn more about ships. I grew up like most other American children—eating pizza, listening to popular tunes on the radio, and attending high-school football games.

I enjoyed different kinds of music, such as classical and pop. I was a member of the J. J. Kelly Indian Marching Band and played clarinet (I wasn't very good at it). We attended various band competitions and with over ninety playing members, we usually received number-one ratings. I tried out for and made drum majorette of the band my senior year. (That was fun!) I even won a first-place award for drum

major in our band's competition. (Boy, was I nervous.)

I graduated from Emory and Henry College with a Bachelor of Arts degree in 1986 and the University of Richmond with a Master's in Reading in 1996. I have taught kindergarten, first, third, and fourth grades and am currently a reading specialist and a children's book author living in Newport News, Virginia. I enjoy watching all of the ships come and go through Hampton Roads. My first book, *Grandfather's Ship, The* SS *United States,* is also about a famous ship!

K. Fact/opinion: A fact can be proven. An opinion is what some one thinks or feels.

    1. Pg. 28, "She wasn't designed to take a blow such as that one especially at her age and with the condition of her hull." (fact/opinion)

    2. Pg. 42, "If you and your friends are going over to the ship, do so before high tide. The currents are very bad here." (fact/opinion)

    3. Pg. 61, "I like her better with two smokestacks and her hull painted black, the top part white and the smokestacks colored red, white and blue." (fact/opinion)

    4. Pg. 69, "It is best to invest your time wisely with people who are receptive and open-minded." (fact/opinion)

    5. Pg. 92, "No matter how much something matters, some one matters more." (fact/opinion)

II. Social Studies

Timelines of historical events: 1939 (when

America was christened) to 1994. Atlas/global studies: Geographic locations mentioned

   A. United States: Virginia—Newport News
   B. Canary Islands: Fuerteventura—Playa de Garcey
   C. Spain
   D. Greece
   E. Thailand
   F. Suez Canal
   G. Africa
   H. Straits of Gibraltar
   I. Australia
   J. New Zealand

III. Technology: Web sites:

www.flare.net / users / e9ee52a / S.S.%20 America.htm

www.homepages.paradise.net.nz / dgriff/

http://uncommonjourneys.com/pages/america.htm

www.gibbscox.com

www.red2000.com / spain / canarias

IV. Science/math:

In Chapter Two, the Díaz family had potato cakes for breakfast. Using your measuring skills from math and your sequencing skills from reading, ask an adult to help you make the following recipe for potato cakes:

- Two cups of leftover homemade mashed potatoes (cooked the night before and refrigerated)
- Four tablespoons of olive oil
- Three tablespoons of plain four
- Salt and pepper to taste
- Cheddar cheese if desired—optional

In an iron skillet, pour four tablespoons of olive oil and place temperature of unit on medium heat. Then mold the leftover potatoes into patty-sized cakes and dust them on both sides with the plain flour. Next, place the cakes into the warm oiled skillet and brown on each side. After the cakes have browned well on both sides, remove from skillet and place on paper towels to absorb any leftover oil. Finally, salt and pepper to taste after placing cakes on plates. Shredded cheddar cheese may be sprinkled on top if desired.

- Remember, *never* cook without adult supervision and permission. You could get burned if someone is not with you.

Physical/chemical changes:

Physical change—are the mashed potatoes changing from one shape or form to another by way of force? Chemical change—is the dusted flour on the outside of the potato cakes changing color, white, to brown by way of the heat and hot oil? Oxidation of iron/steel is another chemical change. Money exchange (dollars for *dinero*).

Spanish Glossary

agua—water
amigo, amiga—friend
barco—boat
bebé—baby
casa—house, home
cena—supper
dinero—money, currency
escuela—school
Estados Unidos—United States
fuego—fire, light
Fuerteventura—one of the Canary Islands
gracias—thank you
gringo—Anglo Saxon, white
hermano—brother, companion
hola—hello
hombre—man
libro—book
loco—mad, crazy
mucho—many, much
Paraja Bridge—Name of area on Fuerteventura.
perro—dog
peces—fish
playa—beach
Puerto Del Rosary-Section of the Island, Fuerteventura
remolcador—tug
señor—mister

señora—lady
siesta—nap
sí—yes
transatlántico—liner, steamer
teléfono—telephone
ventana—window

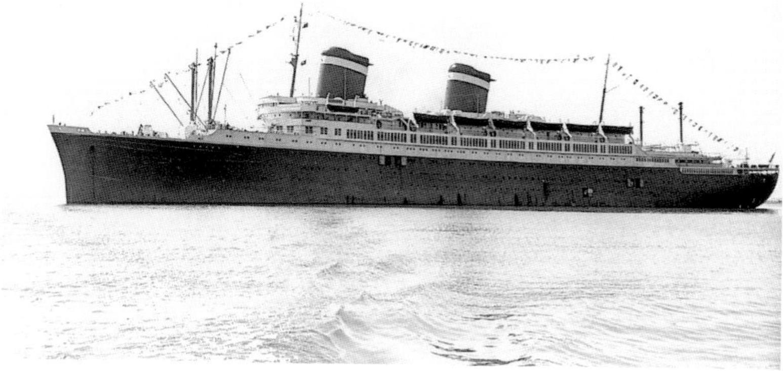

Fletcher Collection